She wasn't sure what she'd say to Matt Dalton. Time had made them strangers.

Swallowing a lump in her throat, she brushed dust from her black silk dress. He'd been at her mother's funeral this morning, but Rachel barely remembered talking with him.

"Mommy, who's that?"

"Someone I used to know."

"Hi, Rachel, I'm real sorry about your mom." The comforting sounds of his deep voice made the years fall away like rich soil beneath the blade of a plow. "Sarah sent this over for your evening meal."

When she took the sack, their fingers brushed. The sudden contact made her pulse quicken. Shaking away the unwanted feelings, she vowed not to let memories ruin this reunion.

Books by Merrillee Whren

Love Inspired

The Heart's Homecoming
An Unexpected Blessing
Love Walked In
The Heart's Forgiveness
Four Little Blessings
Mommy's Hometown Hero

MERRILLEE WHREN

is the winner of the 2003 Golden Heart Award for Best Inspirational Romance manuscript, presented by Romance Writers of America. In 2004, she made her first sale to Steeple Hill. She is married to her own personal hero, her husband of thirty-plus years, and has two grown daughters. She has lived in Atlanta, Boston, Dallas and Chicago, but now makes her home on one of God's most beautiful creations, an island off the east coast of Florida. When she's not writing or working for her husband's recruiting firm, she spends her free time playing tennis or walking the beach, where she does the plotting for her novels. Please visit her Web site at www.merrilleewhren.com.

Mommy's
Hometown Hero
Merrillee Whren

Steeple
Hill®

Published by Steeple Hill Books™

STEEPLE HILL BOOKS

Steeple
Hill®

Recycling programs
for this product may
not exist in your area.

ISBN-13: 978-0-373-87513-9
ISBN-10:   0-373-87513-4

MOMMY'S HOMETOWN HERO

Copyright © 2009 by Merrillee Whren

www.SteepleHill.com

Printed in U.S.A.

But do not forget this one thing, dear friends: with the Lord a day is like a thousand years, and a thousand years are like a day. The Lord is not slow in keeping His promise, as some understand slowness. He is patient with you, not wanting anyone to perish, but everyone to come to repentance.

—*2 Peter* 3:8–9

I would like to dedicate this book to the memory of my grandparents, Ralph and Katherine Merrill and John and Olga Luft, who were South Dakota farmers.

ACKNOWLEDGMENTS

I would like to thank my daughter Danielle and my friend Piper for once again offering your assistance as I wrote this book. I would also like to thank Dr. Judith Boyle for giving me information about post-traumatic stress disorder. Thank you to two South Dakota friends, Janene Kinney and Merlin Tiede, for help with details about farming and South Dakota. I would also like to thank Chip Fowler for information about the National Guard and returning wounded soldiers. All mistakes are mine.

Chapter One

Nothing much had changed in ten years on the farm where Rachel Charbonneau had grown up. The faded red barn sat against a backdrop of fields newly planted with grain and alfalfa. A gentle breeze rustled shiny green leaves in the cottonwoods lining the creek. The peaceful picture didn't tell the whole story. Despite its appeal, she hated this place.

Gripping her daughter's hand, Rachel squinted against the warm May sun in the cloudless sky over the South Dakota prairie. A silver pickup, coming down the lane, bumped across the ground and kicked up a cloud of dust as it came to a stop near the barn. When the driver emerged, she recognized him, even at a distance.

Tightness settled around her heart. Swallowing a lump in her throat, she brushed dust from her black silk dress. She wasn't sure what she would say to Matt Dalton. Time had made them strangers.

With a very obvious limp, Matt trudged toward the barn. His faded jeans and blue chambray shirt with the sleeves rolled up accentuated his tall, muscular build. He'd been at her mother's funeral this morning, among a sea of people who had come to pay their last respects to Lynn Charbonneau, but Rachel barely remembered talking with him. Her mind had been consumed with grief ever since she'd learned her mother had died suddenly in a car accident.

As Matt disappeared into the barn, Becky tugged on Rachel's arm. "Mom, who's that?"

"Someone I used to know." Gazing at her daughter, Rachel wanted to gather Becky close but resisted the protective gesture that had become second nature in the past few weeks. A flush rose in the child's smooth, olive complexion. The breeze ruffled her brown hair lying in natural curls around her shoulders. Rachel brushed the wayward strands from Becky's cheek and wished she could as easily spare her daughter the heartaches of life.

"What's he doing in the barn?" Becky asked.

"I'm not sure."

"Can we go see?"

"No, we aren't dressed for that. We'll check out the barn another time." Rachel figured talking to Matt would come soon enough.

"But I want to go now."

"We'll be here a few days. You can wait." Rachel glanced toward the barn again just as Matt reappeared and retrieved a large sack from his pickup. "Look. Here he comes." Rachel summoned a welcoming smile as he drew closer. "Hello, Matt."

"Hi, Rachel, I'm real sorry about your mom. I didn't get a chance to say more than a few words to you this morning. Had to get back to the fields, so we didn't get to stay for lunch." The comforting sound of his deep voice made the years fall away like rich soil beneath the blade of a plow.

"Thanks." Rachel nodded. "There were so many people. It all seems like a blur."

"I'm sure it does." He stepped forward and held out the sack he carried. "Sarah sent this over for your evening meal."

Was Sarah his wife? Had Matt been with his family this morning? Rachel just couldn't remember. His going off to war and subsequent return as an injured soldier were the only news her mother had ever shared. When Rachel left town, he was engaged but not to someone named Sarah. Rachel had never dared to ask about Matt's marriage, and she couldn't bring herself to ask now.

When she took the sack, their fingers brushed. The sudden contact made her pulse quicken. Shaking away the unwanted feelings, she vowed not to let memories ruin this reunion. Besides, she shouldn't have such feelings for a married man. "You want to come up to the house for a few minutes while I put this in the kitchen? My grandparents would love to talk to you."

Looking back at the barn, Matt hesitated. "Feeding the horses didn't take that long. I can probably spare a few minutes."

"Still teaching school and helping out at the farm in the summer?" Rachel asked, wishing she could ask about his injuries but feeling it was the wrong time for such a discussion.

"Yeah, it's what I love."

Rachel looked at her little girl. Becky was Rachel's love. Nothing was more important in her life, especially now. "This is my daughter. Becky, say hello to Mr. Dalton."

Matt extended his hand to her as she looked up at him. "I'm glad to meet you, Becky. You don't have to call me Mr. Dalton. You can call me Matt. How old are you?"

Smiling shyly, Becky shook his hand. "Almost six."

"Your mom was the same age when I first met her. She used to pal around with me and my cousins when I visited their farm every summer." Matt hunkered down to Becky's eye level. "You look just like your mom when she was a girl."

"No, I don't," Becky said. "She doesn't have blue eyes like me. Hers are brown."

"You're right. Where'd you get those pretty blue eyes?"

"From my dad, but he died before I was born."

"I'm real sorry about that. Where'd your mom get her eyes?"

"From my great, great, great, great grandma. She was a beautiful Sioux Indian princess."

"But not as beautiful as you and your mom." Standing, Matt patted Becky on the head.

Shrugging and gazing at the ground, she sidled up to Rachel. "I guess."

Watching Matt charm her daughter just the way he'd charmed her years ago, Rachel tried to read his tanned features shaded by a ball cap. "I always thought you considered me more of a pest than a pal."

"Well, maybe, but we guys didn't mind having you tag along as much as we let on. Hero worship is good for the ego. And now I can say Rachel Carr, glamorous TV star, spent her summers following me around." Matt winked.

"You exaggerate." Leading the way across the farmyard toward the house, Rachel absorbed the strange sound of her professional name on the lips of a friend. Nothing had prepared her for dealing with the way people from her past thought of her now. Did they think success had gone to her head? Would they treat her differently? She hoped not.

He gave her a lopsided grin and, despite his limp, matched her step as they traversed the uneven ground. "No exaggeration. Your smiling face greets me from the magazine rack of every grocery checkout lane."

"What are the tabloids saying these days?" she asked, pretending she didn't know. The stories they printed were laughable, sometimes irritating and mostly untrue. They often took half-truths and turned them into stories. Now, her mother's death added to her trouble. Would the heartaches never end?

When they reached the patio at the back of the house, Matt

stopped next to a wrought-iron umbrella table. His golden eyes twinkled with amusement. "You're involved with three handsome actors, feuding with your agent and leaving your TV show because you've been diagnosed with some debilitating malady." The twinkle left his eyes. "You aren't really sick, are you?"

"I don't have any debilitating diseases, but…"

"But what?"

The concern in his voice touched her heart. "I'm not doing the TV show next year because I need a rest. Besides, I'm being considered for the lead role in a feature film—something I've always wanted. I don't want anything to keep me from getting that part."

"You'll get it. You've gotten everything else you've wanted in your career."

Rachel could only nod as a bitter lump rose in her throat. His statement reminded her that, despite a successful career, her personal life was full of tragedy. Fame and money could never replace the people she'd lost. "I'm glad you have so much confidence in me. It's too bad you're not making the final decision."

"Mom." Becky gazed up at her. "Can I change my clothes?"

"Sure, tell Grandma and Grandpa we have company." Rachel thought of her mother's parents and their grief over their daughter's death—the grief they all shared.

Lagging behind Becky as she sprinted to the house, Rachel glanced over her shoulder at Matt. He smiled, and her heart skipped just the way it had so many years ago when he'd smiled at her. As they reached the back door, he quickly stepped in front of her and opened it. The courteous gesture reminded her that things were kinder and gentler in the country compared to the big city.

The smell of morning coffee still lingered in the kitchen. The old oak table and chairs were the only familiar things in the room. Blue and white checked curtains, decorating the window over the kitchen sink, matched the chair pads. Gleaming white counters and light oak cabinets had replaced the butcher-block counters and dark pine cabinets she'd known as a child. The changes reminded her that she'd been gone a long time.

"Does this stuff need to go in the refrigerator?"

"Yeah." He let the screen door slap shut behind him as he removed his cap and finger-combed his thick wheat-straw-colored hair. "I see you passed on the family history to your daughter."

Nodding, Rachel removed a white casserole dish from the sack. "It all started over the question of eye color. She wanted to know why her eyes are blue and mine aren't."

"A legitimate question."

Rachel put the dish in the refrigerator, then turned to face Matt. "She asks lots of questions these days. And I don't always have the answers."

Matt chuckled. "Not the birds and bees already."

"No. Life and death," Rachel said, unable to miss the scars on the right side of his face, more visible now that he had removed his baseball cap.

"Tough subjects. I've always found trust in God provides a lot of answers and comfort, too."

Rachel looked at the floor. She didn't want Matt to see the doubt in her eyes. Is that the way he still felt after all he'd been through? Matt had faced death as a soldier and survived. She wondered how he'd managed to keep his faith when her faith in God had died ten years ago along with her father.

Scared and alone in a hospital emergency room, she'd prayed that God would spare her father's life, but the heart attack had killed him. God hadn't helped then. He wasn't helping now. Nothing could dull the pain of her mother's death.

"I suppose you could say that," she mumbled, blinking away her tears.

"Are you all right?" Matt stepped closer and put his arm around her shoulders.

"I'm coping, but I can't always keep the tears from coming." The warmth of his touch made her want to slip into his embrace and shut out the anguish of losing her mother. She had treasured their friendship that had begun when he visited his uncle's farm one summer. He was twelve, and she was just a six-year-old kid with a ponytail and skinned knees.

After his first visit, he came every summer to help on the Dalton farm. The summer after his high school graduation, he came and stayed, going to college at South Dakota State in the fall. He worked on the Dalton farm during the summers until he finished college. Her junior year, he started teaching biology at the local high school.

He patted her shoulder. "I wish I could make it all better."

"Like when I was a teenager." She nodded, remembering how Matt had been there to console her when she'd lost the 4-H competition at the state fair, made her laugh when she didn't get the lead in the school play and had run interference when she'd driven her mother's car into a ditch.

But she had to keep in mind that he wasn't single anymore. A friend was all he'd ever be. Her thoughts came to an abrupt halt when Becky reappeared wearing jeans and a T-shirt.

"Mom, Grandma and Grandpa are resting."

"Then we won't disturb them."

"How long do you plan to stay?" Matt asked.

Rachel shrugged. "I'm not sure."

"It would be great to have you around for a while."

"I don't have definite plans right now. I have some big decisions to make."

"Yes, you do." He stepped toward the door. "I'd better get

going. Say hi to your grandparents. I'll see you at church tomorrow."

"I suppose." Rachel didn't want to tell him she didn't plan to be there.

He pushed open the screen door and stopped. "I'll be praying for you and those decisions you have to make, too."

Stepping outside with Matt, Rachel forced a smile. Could he ever understand she didn't share his faith or reliance on prayer anymore? "Tell your wife thanks for the food."

Matt chuckled as surprise showed on his face. "Sarah's not my wife. She's married to John."

Rachel's heart skipped a beat. "Your cousin?"

"Yeah, I'm just the single deliveryman." Matt grinned. "John would be pretty upset if he thought I was trying to run off with his wife."

"Sorry. I should know better than to jump to conclusions. That's what the tabloid press does all the time."

"No problem." Matt grinned again. "I'll introduce you to Sarah tomorrow. You'll like her. And they have a little girl the same age as Becky."

"Great." Rachel forced another smile. Another reason for her to attend church. The expectations continued to mount.

As Matt drove toward the blacktop road, Rachel stood with Becky at the edge of the patio and waved. A gamut of emotions washed over her. What was there about him that made her remember her painful teenage crush like it was yesterday? Maybe it was the newness of seeing him after all these years, maybe finding out he wasn't married. Or were her emotions all tied up in the death of her mother and the shock of seeing Matt's injuries?

He still had that easy charm, but he carried the physical scars of the combat he'd seen. And his eyes, surrounded by deepened lines, held a look that told her he'd endured too many horrors.

She wondered what changes he saw in her. The unexpected feelings she still had for him made her wary. They were part of the past and connected to this farm, something she wanted out of her life. And he had faith in God, something she couldn't share.

As Rachel turned toward the house, Becky pulled her to a stop. "Why does Matt walk funny and have scars on his face?"

Rachel stared at her daughter. Thankfully, she hadn't asked the question in front of Matt. "He was a soldier and was injured when he fought in the war."

"Does it hurt?"

Reading Becky's look of concern, Rachel wondered how she should answer that question. What kind of pain had he known? Emotional pain often lingered longer than the physical. She could testify to that. "I don't know whether it hurts anymore, honey. But he's a very brave man."

"And he's nice."

Rachel was glad her child could see beyond his physical appearance to the real man beneath the scars. But was he the same as the young man she'd had a crush on as a girl?

Shaking away her troubled thoughts, Rachel walked toward the red brick ranch house that had been her childhood home. She drank in the familiar sight of her favorite childhood haunt—the tree fort sitting on the large limbs of the cottonwood tree closest to the house. The oak and maple trees surrounding the house had flourished in the last ten years. Planting those trees with her father had been one of the last happy memories she had of him before the worry and care of keeping the farm afloat had taken their toll. Now her mother was gone, too. She pressed her lips together to keep from crying.

As Rachel and Becky crossed the patio, a voice sounded from inside the house. "Did I hear a car?"

Rachel glanced toward the back door. Her grandmother,

Kate, stood on the threshold. "Yes, Grandma. You just missed Matt Dalton. He brought something for our supper."

"Sorry I missed him. You should've gotten us," Kate said.

"I didn't want to disturb you."

"I know, but I'd like to have spoken with Matt. He was such a help to your mother. Whenever she needed something, he was here to lend a hand." Kate stepped back into the kitchen as her husband joined her. "It's a shame what that boy's been through."

Rachel nodded. "I didn't realize the extent of his injuries."

"You aren't even seeing the half of it," her grandmother stated. "He almost died."

"I was surprised to learn he'd come back here after he recovered," Rachel said.

"He did spend the summer after his rehab with his folks in Georgia, but he came back as soon as school started. He considers this his home." George Hofer peered at Rachel through his wire-rimmed glasses. "Matt's a fine person. You'd do well to marry someone like him and give that daughter of yours a good father."

Watching Becky skip across the patio, Rachel made no reply. Would she be getting a lecture at every turn on how she should find a father for Becky? After her bad choices when it came to men, Rachel didn't want to think about tying herself to another one, even for Becky.

The aroma of frying bacon filled the air as Rachel approached the kitchen the following morning. Sunday had always meant church when she was growing up. But she hadn't attended church in years, and she wondered how she could avoid going today. "Good morning, Grandma. Grandpa."

Her grandmother glanced up from the stove. "You sound chipper."

"I do feel better."

"Well, the world always looks a little better after a night's rest," Grandpa said. "You still haven't said what you plan to do with the farm."

"Sell it." Sighing deeply, Rachel looked away. While she waited for her grandfather's reply, the clock in the nearby den chimed as if to signal the protest she expected to hear.

Leaning forward, he set his coffee cup on the table. "I think it's sad you have to part with this place. There are lots of good memories here."

The idea of strangers living in this house and caring for the garden was not a pleasant one, but Rachel steeled herself against sentimental feelings. The farm had to go. There was no other way. "I never liked farming. It's a hard way of life. It takes a special kind of person to endure it."

"Farmers love the land and thrive on seeing their crops come in or their livestock taken to market."

"To me, they're gluttons for punishment who watch months of work destroyed by a hailstorm, tornado or drought." She closed her eyes and pinched the bridge of her nose. "I don't know how they do it or why, especially when they don't survive."

"Are you talking about your father?" Her grandfather stood and put an arm around her shoulders.

"This farm killed him."

"Is that why you're so determined to sell it?"

"No, I'm selling it because I have no use for a farm. You're not going to talk me out of it. I have a life in California. Not here."

Grandpa patted her shoulder. "You have to do what's best for you, but give yourself time to think things over before you make any major decisions."

Smiling wryly, Rachel shook her finger at him. "Grandpa,

you're playing games with me. You're telling me what I do is my business, but underneath this agreeable attitude you're trying to undermine my decision." She watched while he opened his mouth in protest. "Don't try to weasel out of it."

"How dare you doubt my intentions!" He chuckled. "Humor an old man and give staying here some thought. It would be a good place to take the time off you've been talking about. I know when Grandma and I go back home, it would be a load off our minds if we knew someone was here to look after the place."

"I'm not deciding anything today."

"That's reasonable, but you'd better get ready for church because we're invited to the Daltons' for Sunday dinner," Grandma said, wiping her hands on her apron. "We'll be going right after church."

Rachel's stomach knotted at the thought of going back to the church she'd attended as a child. "I wasn't planning to go. I wanted to start going through Mom's things."

Grandma stopped turning the bacon and studied her. The snap and pop of the hot grease filled the silence. "You ought to go this morning. A lot of people are expecting you."

"I don't want to be a hypocrite. Church just isn't for me anymore." Rachel crossed her arms at her waist. "Grandma, when good people like my parents die in the prime of their lives, doesn't it shake your faith in God? How can you trust in a God who would allow this to happen?"

"Rachel, I know how your father's death affected you, and I'm sure your husband's and now your mother's deaths have done nothing to change your attitude about God. But your grandfather's and my faith isn't shaken by the death of a loved one, even though we don't always understand why it happened. I trust God to know what's best, and that, in His wisdom, all things will work out for those who believe in Him."

Tears welled in Rachel's eyes as she gazed out the kitchen window. Blinking, she tried to gain control of her emotions. "I sometimes envy your faith, but I can't believe anymore. The world seems to go on without any sign of a superior being in control."

"I'm not trying to convince you to believe. I know your mother tried to restore your faith, but she realized you would have to make that decision on your own. About the only thing we can do is what your mother always did. Pray."

Rachel kept her eyes focused on the view out the kitchen window and slowly shook her head. "I don't think your prayers will do much good."

Her grandmother put her hand on Rachel's shoulder. "The Bible says, 'The fervent prayer of a righteous man is powerful and effective.' We plan to continue praying for you every day."

"I know I can't stop you. And I suppose you're right. I should go this morning to honor my mother." Rachel's stomach lurched. A command performance for all of the relatives and friends—one of the reasons she'd never wanted to come back.

Chapter Two

With trepidation, Rachel made the trip to the little country church where she would face not only her relatives again, but also reminders of her mother's death. As Grandpa stopped the car along the blacktop road, Rachel felt her heart flutter.

Sun glinted off the stained glass windows, and the steeple rose against the bright blue sky. But even the beauty of the white clapboard building set among the elm trees didn't keep Rachel from seeing the flowers still lying on the plot where her parents were now buried side by side in the church cemetery.

"Mom, is that Matt?"

Becky's question took Rachel's attention away from the heartwrenching scene. She looked to where Becky was pointing. "Yes. That's Matt."

Becky began wildly waving her hands over her head. Matt caught sight of them as he and his cousin John walked across the churchyard toward the concrete staircase leading to the church's big wooden door. Grinning, he waved back.

Becky tugged on Rachel's arm. "He sees us."

Rachel chuckled at Becky's excitement over seeing him again. "Looks like he's waiting for us."

"Will I get to meet that girl with him?"

"I'm sure he'll introduce us," Rachel said, noticing the woman with light brown hair, a plump face and kind smile. She held the hand of a little girl about Becky's age.

"I hope so." Becky skipped ahead.

Rachel marveled that her normally shy daughter was so eager to meet someone new. "Becky, wait for me."

"Hurry, Mom."

Rachel met Matt's gaze. He smiled and a tingle of anticipation rippled through her. Why did feelings from the past keep reemerging?

"Hello, Becky." Matt's smile widened into a grin. "I want you to meet Erin." He ushered the little girl with the honey-colored hair forward.

The little girls exchanged timid greetings while Matt introduced Rachel to Sarah.

Sarah shook Rachel's hand. "Wow! I can hardly believe I'm talking with Rachel Carr. You seem like a regular person."

"Well, I hope so." Rachel laughed, but she sensed uneasiness in Sarah's comment. Rachel *did* want Sarah to see her as a regular person, not some TV personality. What would it take to get everyone to see beyond her professional persona?

Sarah grimaced. "I'm sorry. I didn't mean to gush. It's just...well, you're the first famous person I've ever met."

Chuckling, John glanced at his wife. "I watched Rachel grow up. Just think of her as the girl next door." He gave Rachel a big hug. "It's good to have you home."

"Thanks. It's good to see you again. Even though I saw you yesterday, it's still all a blur." Rachel realized coming back here might not be as bad as she'd anticipated.

"It'll take you a while to get through the grieving process. We're all going to miss your mom." John tapped his daughter on the arm. "Erin, please show Becky where your class is."

"Okay, Dad." Erin grabbed Becky's hand. "Follow me."

"See you later, Mom." Becky darted away with Erin without a backward glance. Giggling, they bounded up the wide church steps and slipped through the door.

"The girls have become fast friends," Sarah said.

"It looks that way." Rachel stood in disbelief at the way Becky had taken to Erin after such a brief encounter.

"It's too bad you can't stay for awhile. Erin would love to have Becky for a playmate. There are very few girls her age around here."

"Yeah." Rachel's reply was barely audible as they climbed the steps. Was everyone conspiring to get her to stay?

When they walked into the vestibule, John draped an arm around Sarah's shoulders. Grandpa and Grandma Hofer held hands. Rachel smiled at the sight.

Matt grinned. "Looks like I'm stuck with you again. Just like old times."

Rachel looked at him with mock indignation. "You could do worse."

"Much worse," he whispered in her ear as they settled into a pew beside her grandparents.

Matt's whisper made her heart pound. The sound echoed in her brain, threatening to drown out the gregarious talking around them. Surely he couldn't hear it.

These feelings were crazy. It had been ten years since she'd even seen him. She'd moved away and fallen in love with someone else, but love had been a disappointment. She didn't have any desire to go down that path again.

The congregation quieted when her uncle Henry walked to the front of the auditorium to lead the adult Bible class. He stepped behind the ornately carved pulpit, stained in a deep walnut color that matched the woodwork throughout the old building. While the world around them had changed, few things had changed in this little country church. Time seemed to have stood still.

Rachel paid little attention to the church service. Thoughts of Matt filled her mind. His presence heightened all of her senses. When he reached for the hymnal and indicated she could share it with him, she watched his strong, tanned hands holding the book. But she didn't miss the very visible scars.

He shifted in his seat and put his arm along the back of the pew behind her. Prickles of excitement pulsed through her. Were these feelings only a remnant of a schoolgirl crush? They would be of little concern if she weren't thinking about spending more time here. What would happen if she decided to stay for the summer?

Throughout the church service her mind wandered back across her school years to how she'd anticipate Matt's annual summer visit and wish with all her being that she were older. Even though Matt and his cousins would include her in their summer fun, what teenaged boy was going to look at a little girl six years younger as anything other than a nuisance?

Matt, with his sun-bleached hair and golden eyes, had filled her girlish dreams. She'd never stopped dreaming that one day he would discover she was no longer a little girl. But her hopes had been dashed during her Christmas break her freshman year in college when she came home to find Matt engaged. She hadn't grown up fast enough. Trading her dreams of Matt for dreams of an acting career, she headed to California the following summer.

What had happened to keep him from marrying Amy? Now Rachel's dream that he would no longer see her as the girl who was too tall and too skinny had come true, but ten years too late. Maybe it had always been too late.

After the last note of the closing hymn sounded, Rachel stood beside Matt and greeted her relatives and folks she'd known for years. She'd seen them at the funeral, when they'd offered their heartfelt condolences. Now they wanted to know what she was going to do with the farm. They meant well but had no idea she didn't welcome their inquiries. These were decisions she wasn't ready to face.

As Rachel hugged another one of her aunts, Grandma Hofer approached. "Rachel, we need to get going. John and Sarah are expecting us."

Glad to be rescued for the moment, Rachel gave Aunt Lois a peck on the cheek. "Gotta go. We'll talk another time."

"You should come to ladies' circle. We meet on Tuesdays," Aunt Lois said.

"We'll see." Forcing a smile, Rachel contemplated the invitation she didn't want to accept. "Bye."

With good-byes and well wishes ringing in her ears, Rachel followed her grandmother out to the car. Now she had to face another invitation—Sunday dinner with the Daltons. The thought of more time with Matt had her stomach full of butterflies.

This shouldn't be happening. She wasn't a kid anymore. She was a grown woman with a child. So why was she having the same fluttery feelings she'd had as a girl about a man she hadn't seen in ten years?

Matt slowly drove his pickup down the gravel lane lined with poplar trees. When he stopped in front of the white clapboard farmhouse nestled among the old elm trees, Rachel's grandfather parked his big black sedan at the edge of the yard. Becky catapulted from the car and joined Erin in a dash across the lawn. Then Rachel stepped out of the car, her black and white dress ruffled around her legs in the breeze.

He studied her as she and her grandparents moseyed toward the house. She stopped on the stoop and turned to watch Becky and Erin play on the tire swing. Her dark hair hung in a French braid down the middle of her back. Her high cheekbones and smooth olive complexion with a hint of roses in her cheeks were made for the camera. Ebony eyes added a touch of mystery to her beauty.

Seeing her today, he couldn't believe he'd held her in a comforting embrace just yesterday. She'd been little Rachel Charbonneau, grieving for her mother. Now all he saw was Rachel Carr, famous actress, and she made him nervous.

Gripping the steering wheel, he tried to tell himself her fame shouldn't make a difference in their relationship. He should think of her as his friend. But there had been a ten-year gap in that friendship.

A lot of crazy emotions wound their way through his acquaintance with Rachel. The little girl he'd first met during his summertime visits had grown into a tall gangly teenager with braces by the time he graduated from college and came to teach in his adopted hometown. All those years he'd befriended her.

Then she graduated from high school. Suddenly she was a young woman, and he realized his feelings didn't stop at friendship. But he'd never considered acting on those feelings, because she was eighteen and he was twenty-four. Their relationship had always been friend and teacher, and he figured it best that it stayed that way. But thoughts of her had never been far away, even in the bleakest days of his recovery from his wartime injuries.

Now she was back, and surprisingly, those long-buried feelings had resurrected themselves. Still, he couldn't act on them. He was a broken man. Most of the time he didn't think about the scars marring his face. Even the limp didn't bother him most days, but emotional scars lingered.

How many nights had he awakened, soaked in sweat, from

a horrific dream? The blinding explosion and pain would come rushing back. He'd spent months in counseling to overcome the terrors of war. Besides, a famous TV star wouldn't have an interest in a scarred schoolteacher. He put that thought firmly in his mind as he stepped out of his pickup.

As he walked across the yard, trying his best not to limp, Rachel looked his way. He forced a smile, but he couldn't push away his self-consciousness. "Hi."

"So you decided to join us? I was beginning to think you were going to stay in your pickup."

Matt shook his head and motioned toward the two little girls. "Just watching them play. Becky reminds me of another little girl I used to know."

"Who?"

Matt gave her a sideways glance. "You know who I mean. The little girl who used to try so hard to fit in with all of us rowdy boys."

Stopping, Rachel turned to look at him. "Are you saying I was a tomboy?"

"No, but you certainly had a mind of your own. No one was going to tell you that you couldn't keep up with the boys."

"And I haven't changed."

"I'm beginning to see that already," Matt said, his nervousness slowly slipping away.

"You live here on the farm now?"

Matt nodded. "I moved out here after my aunt and uncle retired to Arizona. That way I'm here to lend John a hand if he needs one. Before my National Guard unit was called up, I helped John remodel this place, so he and Sarah could move in here."

"Then you live in the big house by yourself?"

"Yeah, just me and the mice."

Rachel laughed, and her laughter went a long way toward

lifting his spirits. Maybe he *really* could think of her as his friend. Why was he concerned? She was only going to be here for a short time.

Rachel called to Becky and Erin, and they joined her as they followed Matt into the kitchen where Sarah was already busy bringing dishes out of the cupboard. The delicious smell of pot roast filled the air.

"Sarah, is there something I can do to help?" Rachel asked.

"You and Matt can take these into the dining room." Sarah handed Matt a platter laden with the roast, potatoes and carrots. She gave Rachel a bowl of green beans.

As Rachel put the beans on the table, Becky and Erin raced into the room and claimed their seats. Matt set the platter down and took the chair beside Rachel. He remembered the Sunday dinners he'd eaten with the Dalton clan over the years and wondered how Rachel felt about being here, especially when they joined hands to pray.

Holding her soft hand in his callused, scarred one reminded him that their lives were worlds apart. He'd be absolutely crazy to think of letting long-ago feelings occupy his mind. He forced himself to concentrate on John's prayer.

After the prayer ended, Sarah handed Rachel the platter. "I'm so glad you could take time to have dinner with us."

"It's my pleasure." Rachel helped herself to some of the roast, then turned to Matt. "How are your parents and brothers?"

Matt hesitated as he thought of his younger brother's trials and how his parents had suffered worrying about two of their sons. But God had brought them through it.

"I hope they're doing okay," Rachel said, when he didn't answer immediately.

"They are, but Mom and Dad had a rough few years helping me recover from my injuries, and then helping Wade deal with Hodgkin's disease."

A little pucker appeared between her eyebrows. "Oh, I'm so sorry. How's he doing?"

"He's in remission and has a new job. He's back out there hugging trees again."

"That's good news." Rachel laughed. "So in a sense he's a farmer, too. His crop's just very, very big."

"Yeah, maybe farming *is* in our genes. It just skipped a generation." Matt chuckled. "But then there's Peter. He's some bigwig in a construction outfit in Atlanta, and I doubt you'd ever get him on a farm again. He never liked coming here when we were kids."

Becky narrowed her gaze as she looked at Matt. "Why does your brother hug trees?"

The adults at the table broke into laughter. Matt patted Becky on the head. "It's only an expression. He works with a company that grows trees, used to make paper and other products."

Sarah glanced at Rachel. "And there's more good news about Wade, although I don't think Matt and Peter want to acknowledge that one of them is finally tying the knot."

Rachel turned to Matt. "Wade's getting married?"

"Yeah. Little brother is the first one of us to bite the dust." Matt grinned. "When he started his new job last summer, he met his soon-to-be wife, Cassie."

Sarah set her fork on the table. "And it's such a cute story."

"How's that?" Rachel asked.

"Well, she's taking care of her two nieces and two nephews, who'd been thrust into foster care because of a bad family situation. The kids were matchmakers for Wade and Cassie. Now they're adopting the kids."

"Wow! That's a big undertaking."

"Yeah, he has a ready-made family." Matt grabbed the platter and helped himself to some more roast.

Sarah looked at Rachel with anxiety written on her face. "Thanks again for joining us today."

Rachel smiled. "I should be the one thanking you."

Chuckling, John gave Sarah a sideways glance, then looked at Rachel. "Sarah can't get over having a celebrity at her table. I'll have to get out some of our old photos. Then she'll see the way we remember you."

"That's a good idea," Matt said, thinking the photos would remind him that she was only a friend.

"Mom, I wanna see them, too."

Rachel laughed, but that little frown puckered her eyebrows again. "I'm not so sure I like that idea. I was shy, and I hated how I looked when I was a kid—all knees and elbows."

Matt grinned. "But those knees and elbows are famous now."

"I can remember when Rachel was a little girl. She was always singing a song or putting on a play with her dolls and stuffed animals," John said. "I never thought you were shy."

"I was. But when I was performing, I was someone else. The first time I stepped onto a stage in elementary school and lost myself in my part in the school play, the applause made me realize I wanted to entertain."

"You surprised everyone when you took off for Hollywood, but not me," John declared. "I knew you'd make it big."

"Sure, you can say that now, since she's a star," Sarah said.

"John told me." Matt looked from Sarah to Rachel. "He tried to convince me you'd do well."

"So you thought I wouldn't make it?" Rachel gave Matt a questioning glance.

Matt cringed inwardly. He'd really stuck his foot in his mouth this time. How was he going to get out of that statement? "I was just worried a sweet farm girl might get swallowed up by that cutthroat business."

"Well, I made it—"

"And we're all glad you did," Matt said as quickly as he could.

After dinner everyone went outside to enjoy the warm, sunny afternoon. Sitting on a lawn chair in the shade of the elms, Rachel watched Matt lean against a tree. While he talked with John and Grandpa, a slight breeze ruffled Matt's thick, golden hair. Her fingers itched to comb it back in place. Clenching her hand, she willed the feeling away. She didn't have the strength to deal with any more emotional upheaval.

Rachel turned her attention to Becky and Erin, who had changed into shorts and T-shirts. They skipped across the yard in the shade of the blue spruce and poplar trees growing along the north side of the house. Rachel remembered how many times she'd done the same thing.

"Mom." Becky's breathless voice disturbed Rachel's musings. "Erin wants to know if I can go over to Matt's house to see the kittens. Can I, Mom, *ple…ease?*"

Rachel smiled at her daughter's pleading. "I suppose, but I'll go with you."

"All right!" Becky and Erin chorused.

"Lead the way."

Rachel walked with the girls down the long drive past the garden on their way to Matt's house. When they neared the fence, the girls skipped ahead and entered through the gate. A minute later, Rachel stepped inside. The large elms surrounding the house made the yard shady and cool. The earthy scent of late spring filled the air.

On their hands and knees, the youngsters looked through a hole in the latticework trim underneath the porch that wrapped around two sides of the white clapboard farmhouse. Crouching behind them, Rachel saw five small bundles of fur curled up together next to their mother.

"They were born a few weeks ago," Erin whispered, looking up at Rachel. "Matt says we can only look at them now. When they're older, he said I can have one."

Rachel knew what was coming, even before Becky spoke.

"Mom, I want a kitten, too."

Rachel shook her head. "We probably won't be here when they're old enough to leave their mother."

"Oh, Mom, can't we stay long enough for me to get a kitten?"

Even Becky was making it hard for her to turn her back on this place. "I don't know, honey. I can't make any promises."

Chapter Three

Standing near the gate, Matt heard Becky's plea. Her words echoed his thoughts. He shouldn't hope for that, but he couldn't help himself. He wished Rachel would stay. He finally admitted it to himself. The idea was crazy, but there it was, permeating his every thought.

When Rachel stood, he shook away his apprehension and approached the trio. "You should listen to your daughter."

Rachel turned. "Eavesdropping?"

"Maybe." Matt glanced at Rachel. "Becky's got a great idea. You said you were taking some time off. I know this isn't the kind of place you jetsetters usually think of when you take vacations, but it would be a change of pace."

"You sound like Grandpa."

"How's that?"

"He thinks I should stay, too."

"Great minds think alike." How could he convince her to take her grandfather's advice? He reminded himself that she wasn't the young girl next door any more. She was a famous TV star. What would she see in a man scarred for life by war? Even if he were whole, would someone like her be interested in an ordinary man like him? What chance did he have with a celebrity?

"Spending my time off here won't change my mind about selling." Her eyes narrowed. "Grandpa said John's been renting the land. How will my selling affect him? Is it a problem?"

"No. Besides, the new owner may want to rent it." Matt hunkered down to eye level with Becky. Her big blue eyes stared back at him, reminding him that Rachel had loved someone else. What had Becky's father been like? Trying to wipe thoughts of the past from his mind, Matt gave Becky a wink. "What would it take to convince your mom to stick around?"

Becky smiled shyly and shrugged. "She wants to be in a movie. Can you put her in a movie?"

Matt chuckled. "I have a good video camera." He glanced up. "Well, what do you say, Rachel?"

"This is all so sudden." She feigned indecision as she put the back of her hand to her forehead in a dramatic pose. "I'll have to think it over."

"You girls can play in the tree house and give me some time to convince your mom to stay." Matt gave Becky another wink.

"Okay," the girls chorused as they sprinted toward the elm tree at the side of Matt's house.

Matt motioned toward the front porch. "Let's sit on the porch swing. We'll have a good view of the girls from there."

"I don't remember that tree house." Rachel stopped at the bottom of the steps leading up to the porch.

"John built it a couple of years ago. Lots of things have changed since you left."

"Yeah, I've noticed. I was surprised John's the only one of your cousins to stay on the farm."

"Paul never came back after college, and Jim moved to the Minneapolis area about four years ago. He was never happy on the farm. Neither was his wife, Mary. She's a city girl."

As Matt climbed the steps, he had to acknowledge Rachel was now a "city girl," too. His former fiancée had taught him city girls don't like country life. But Rachel had once been a country girl, and the thought of having her here for a little while wouldn't leave his mind.

Rachel followed Matt onto the porch and contemplated what spending time on the farm might mean for her. Would there be constant reminders of her parents? Could she cope? She just didn't know the answers. Besides, it was time to quit dwelling on herself and start thinking of others—starting with Matt. Was he willing to talk about his injuries?

Rachel joined Matt on the swing. "I was surprised to hear you'd come back."

"Why?"

"I thought you'd stay near your parents in Georgia."

"I thought I might, too, but when I finished my rehab, I missed my teaching job here and the farm. Besides, John needed my help. I'm surprised your mom didn't tell you Paul and Jim left." Matt put his arm along the back of the swing as he sprawled his legs out in front of him.

Rachel tried to focus her thoughts on something other than the way Matt's nearness sent her stomach spinning. "Mom probably tried to tell me lots of things, but I didn't want to listen."

"Why?"

She looked away from his questioning gaze. "I wanted to forget everything about this place. Too many bad memories."

"They're not all bad."

"But when they were bad, they were awful." The losses in her life threatened to overwhelm her. She pushed aside the negative thoughts. "I know you love it here."

He smiled wryly. "Yeah. This place has become a part of me. I suspect you don't understand why."

Rachel checked on the girls, finding an excuse not to look at Matt. She didn't want him to see the truth in her eyes. She didn't understand what drew him here. Why did he enjoy working on a farm when he really didn't have to? Even though he taught school to earn a living, he loved the land—just like her father.

She gripped the swing's chain until the links bit into her hand. Even after hating this place all these years, she still felt the pull of the wide-open spaces—where you could see forever.

"It's important to like what you do and where you live," she finally replied.

"Why did you stay away?" Matt shifted sideways in his seat until he was facing her from the opposite end of the swing.

Weighing her words, she said, "I hated what the farm did to my dad. It killed him because he wouldn't give it up."

"So you think I'm crazy to help John and Sarah with the farm in addition to teaching?"

She smiled slightly. "Hey, I can't make any judgments. I play make-believe for a living. You have to do what's right for you."

"Staying away for ten years was right for you?" His tawny gaze intensified as he waited for her answer.

"It was at the time."

"Now you're not sure?"

She shrugged. "I don't know. I was angry for a long time over my father's death. And there were all these people back here who expected me to be something I couldn't be anymore. I didn't want to deal with it." She ran one hand along the back of the swing.

"And what did people expect you to be?"

Releasing a long sigh, she realized she'd never voiced her doubts aloud, not even to her mother. She'd harbored them deep in her heart until they'd pushed every thought of God from her mind. "Little Rachel Charbonneau attending church, singing in the choir, or praying for the sick. I couldn't pretend to do those things anymore and mean them. I would've been playing a part. Not like you."

"How's that?"

"You always did the right thing. You went to war when your country called and came back a hero. You're a respected teacher, doing work you love. You've lived up to everyone's expectations. I didn't."

Rachel felt Matt's scrutiny as she rose from the swing and walked to the balustrade surrounding the porch. A lilac bush grew nearby. Leaning over, she buried her face in a fluffy purple bloom and drank in the familiar fragrance.

Matt followed her as she sat on the balustrade railing. "Are you kidding? You exceeded everyone's expectations. I still don't understand why you stayed away for ten years. Your mom said you were too busy to come home."

"I was."

Looking down, he rubbed the back of his neck. "People were concerned that you never came to visit your mother."

"After she retired from teaching, she was free to visit me any time. I thought she enjoyed spending the winter months in California. Now everyone tells me how much she wanted me to come back here, but she never said so. If she had, I would've come."

"I'm sure you would have."

Rachel didn't want him to think badly of her. Did he really mean what he said, or was he only being polite? As she gazed into his golden eyes, she realized for all those years she hadn't been worried about what her relatives or friends would think, but what Matt would. Now he knew the truth—she didn't share his faith anymore. "I just thought it was easier for her to visit me." Rachel lowered her gaze. "And I wouldn't have to pretend to care about God. I've drifted too far from God to ever come back."

A long silence ensued as she waited for his response. She slid down from the railing, walked around the corner to the front porch and looked out across the drive toward the barn and fields. Uneven footsteps announced his approach. He placed a hand on her shoulder. "You're never too far away."

She turned to look at him. Could he tell the way his touch made her heart beat a little faster? His presence made her legs feel as weak as one of the newborn kittens. She was that young girl again with a bad case of puppy love. Hoping to put an end to her foolish emotions, she said, "That's not the way I feel right now. It's not the way I've felt in years. Don't try to change my mind."

Matt sighed. "Well, if I can't change your mind about God, at least, let me change your mind about the farm. Don't sell. You'll regret it."

"I don't have a choice."

"Yes, you do. You don't have to sell. Your mother didn't farm this land."

"But she lived here. I'm not going to live here. So what would be the point in keeping this place?" She raised her hands in frustration.

"It's your family's heritage."

"I know. But even if I keep it, chances are it would pass out of our hands in the next generation. Just look at what's happened right here. Who's going to carry on the Dalton farm after you and John are gone?"

"Erin."

"What are the chances she'll want to stay on the farm?"

"I don't know, but the Daltons have farmed this land for generations. And as long as I'm alive it'll be Dalton land. My dad may not have had an interest in farming, but I do. Even though

I didn't grow up here, I felt at home on every visit. I could hardly wait to come back each summer." Matt's eyes conveyed a fierce determination.

"You have the conviction to keep the land, and I don't," Rachel replied, knowing his resolve meant their thoughts were worlds apart.

"Just don't make any rash decisions. Think of the improvements your mother made with the money you sent her."

"Funny you'd mention that. I gave Mom the money because I knew she'd enjoy remodeling the house, but I've heard whispers that I gave her money instead of my time." Rachel gazed at Matt, challenging him to deny he'd heard the same gossip.

Matt slowly shook his head. "People who say that stuff don't know you very well."

Rachel's heart lifted. "I wanted her to have some luxuries in life. Living on a farm can be so hard. Mom's teaching salary was mainly what we lived on before Dad died. Working our farm brought nothing but heartache."

"I know you feel that way, Rachel, but it can also be rewarding. Don't discard the things your mother treasured."

Closing her eyes, Rachel covered her face with her hands. She willed the hurt and confusion to go away. Finally, she looked at Matt. "She may have treasured it, but I don't. As far as I'm concerned, the farm doesn't need to stay in my family."

Taking her in his arms, he held her close. "I'm so sorry, Rachel. I didn't mean to bring up bad memories. But I still think you'll regret it if you sell. Give it some time. Promise me you'll think it over before you decide."

Encircled in Matt's arms, Rachel only nodded. Laying her head on his shoulder, she drank in the strength and comfort of his embrace. Peace enveloped her. Yet, underneath, an awareness she couldn't deny bubbled around the edges of her heart.

She didn't want to care. Resurrecting her old feelings for Matt would only lead to heartache. Their lifestyles and their ambitions were too different. She couldn't let her heart rule her head.

He slowly released her. "Well, whatever you decide, I'm glad you're here now."

"Me, too," she said, feeling the warmth of his words. "We'd better head back to John and Sarah's."

"Sure."

Going over to the tree, Rachel called the girls. After much protest, they came down. As Rachel walked with Matt, her thoughts turned. Should she follow his advice and spend some time here? This place offered something she needed right now—a refuge from a life that was increasingly chaotic.

When they reached John and Sarah's house, Sarah greeted them from the back porch. "Rachel, your grandparents went on home. I think your grandpa was getting sleepy."

Chuckling, Rachel nodded. "He likes his afternoon nap."

"Anyway," Sarah continued, "John's gone to do the chores, and he's volunteered Matt to take you and Becky home."

"Sounds good to me," Matt said. "Let me change into some work clothes, and I'll feed the horses while I'm there."

While Rachel changed into a pair of jeans, she glanced around her childhood room. Memories occupied every corner. A big box containing keepsakes from her school days sat on the shelf above the rod in the closet. She took down one of the old posters rolled up beside the box. When she unrolled it, she came face to face with the New Kids on the Block. Now she was Rachel Carr, famous television star, and she had her own poster. But being famous wasn't going to bring her mother back.

Tears stung the backs of her eyelids as she heard the small voice of her daughter. "Mommy, what's wrong?"

"I was feeling sad because I won't be able to see Grandma Lynn anymore." Rachel quickly wiped the mist from her eyes.

"That's not true. Grandma Kate says we'll see her again in Heaven."

Nodding, Rachel viewed the bright optimism on her daughter's face and gave her a quick squeeze. "Yes, that's what Grandma Kate believes," Rachel said, not knowing how else to respond without dashing Becky's hopes.

Becky raced toward the bedroom door. "Can we look at the horses now?"

"Sure."

Passing through the den, Rachel surveyed the place where she'd grown up. The well-worn sofa and chair reminded her of the happy times she'd spent with her parents in that very room. She went to the curio cabinet and opened the door.

"What's in there?" Becky came to stand beside her.

"Things your grandma Lynn collected." Rachel picked up a porcelain bell. She cradled its smooth coolness in her hands, then gently shook it. A soft tinkling sound broke the silence. A tear trickled down her cheek. She quickly wiped it away, hoping Becky wouldn't see her crying again. "I gave this to your Grandma Lynn one Christmas."

"It's pretty, but let's go." Becky pulled her mother toward the sliding glass door next to the fireplace.

Rachel quickly put the bell back into the curio and followed Becky outside. Squinting against the sun, she looked toward the barn. The old place had a nostalgic appeal. Should she keep it? Shaking her head, she was determined to enjoy the day. No decisions, no demands. As they made their way toward the barn, the gravel crunching beneath her shoes gave way to dusty ground.

The apple trees and chokecherry bushes stood to the right of the barn. Memories of hot apple pies and chokecherry jelly flooded her mind. She smiled ruefully, realizing her anxiety about returning home had eclipsed all of the pleasant memories.

The smell of hay and animals greeted Rachel as she followed Becky into the barn's dim light. Dust motes swirled in the beam of sunlight shining through the open door. After Rachel's eyes adjusted to the dusky light, she saw Matt hard at work.

With each toss of the pitchfork, his muscles rippled beneath his T-shirt. Taking a deep breath, she tried to think of something other than the way watching him made her pulse quicken.

"Cleaning out the stalls, I see." Rachel wrinkled her nose. "Not one of my favorite jobs."

Matt turned and leaned on the pitchfork. "You two took your sweet time. I'm almost finished."

"I'd say we timed it just right."

"Mom, where are the horses?"

"They're out in the corral behind the barn."

"Can I see them?"

"Sure." Matt smiled and held out a couple of carrots. "You can give these to them."

"Thanks." Becky grabbed the carrots and raced toward the back door of the barn.

Rachel followed Matt toward the corral and marveled at her daughter's fearlessness as a dark brown horse and another one with gray coloring ambled over to inspect the visitors.

Matt leaned over and whispered, "She's certainly excited."

Unable to speak, Rachel nodded. Matt's nearness was doing crazy things to her insides again. She wanted to ignore it, but she couldn't.

After Becky finished giving the horses their treat, the three-some walked back through the barn.

Becky pointed to a ladder. "Mom, what's up there?"

"That's the hayloft. Wanna go up?"

"Yeah."

Carefully, Matt and Rachel followed Becky up the rugged ladder.

"When I was a little girl, I used to spend hours up here playing all sorts of games."

"Cool." Becky jumped into the soft piles of hay.

While Becky entertained herself, Rachel walked over to the loft door, viewing the farm from the heightened vantage point. The branches of the trees along the drive waved in the breeze. The sun glinted off the windows of the house. Everything invited her to stay.

Matt joined her. "The old farm looks pretty good from up here, doesn't it?"

"I can't argue."

"Does that mean you're going to stay for a while?"

Sighing, Rachel shook her head. "No."

"Not even for a few weeks?"

"I'll be here long enough to settle the estate." Thoughts of staying were foolish. The sooner she was gone, the better it would be. But she couldn't deny this was the perfect refuge. Her face was familiar to the millions who watched her on one of television's top rated shows. What better place could she find solace than on a farm in eastern South Dakota? Could she turn her back on this ready-made sanctuary?

Becky came to stand next to them and pointed out the door. "Hey, Mom, is that another tree house?"

"Yes, it's my old tree house."

"Let's go see it," Becky begged.

"Okay."

On their way, they passed through the garden. At the far end, Rachel showed Becky the strawberries and raspberries. Rachel remembered how she'd helped pick berries as a little girl, eating almost as many as she picked.

"Becky, one summer when I was visiting, your mom ate so many raspberries she made herself sick." An impish grin crossed Matt's face.

"Did you really, Mom?"

"Yes." Rachel glanced at Matt with irritation. "He should tell you all the rotten things he did."

"Like what? You were telling me earlier how perfect I was. Can't get your stories straight?"

"I forgot about the summer you and your brothers and cousins knocked over Pearson's outhouse."

"What's an outhouse?" Becky asked.

Rachel looked at Matt. "Are there any around these days?"

"Your Uncle Henry's still got one," Matt said.

Becky put her hands on her hips. "Tell me what it is."

"It's an outdoor toilet in a little house," Rachel said.

Becky immediately turned to Matt. "Will you show me the outhouse?"

"Sure, but another day." He glanced up and grinned at Rachel, then at Becky, whose shyness had evaporated into the warm spring air. "Let's go look at that tree house now."

As they left the barn, Rachel listened to Becky pepper Matt with questions about the horses. Rachel couldn't help remembering how every summer he'd tolerated her tag-along curiosity. Was that what his grin had been about? He remembered, too?

When they reached the tree, Rachel gave Becky a boost up to the first step of the ladder nailed to the trunk. They slowly climbed the ladder and hoisted themselves onto the weathered boards comprising the floor. A crude balustrade surrounded the platform. She walked to the edge. Matt came to stand beside her.

Rachel glanced at Matt. "I'd forgotten how good the view is from up here."

"You've forgotten lots of good things about this place."

"Yeah." Rachel turned to look at Becky, who was gazing around in amazement at the old hideaway.

"Hey, Mom, this is cool. It's even better than the one at Matt's house. Can I play up here?"

"You may come here anytime you want as long as you let me know."

"She likes it here." Matt looked at her with a knowing smile. "Don't be in such a hurry to leave."

Rachel sighed heavily. "At this point, I'm taking it one day at a time."

"Good." He put one arm around her shoulders.

Closing her eyes, Rachel willed herself not to be affected by his persuasive words or the way his touch sent a curling sensation through her. Just this simple gesture threatened her peace of mind.

Finally she turned to look at him. "I have a lot of things to sort out."

"I'll be here to help." He squeezed her shoulder.

"I know." *You're one of things I have to figure out.*

"Mom, let's go swimming."

"You want to join us?" Rachel asked Matt.

He shook his head. "I've got work to do."

"Okay, maybe another time," Rachel said, disappointment flitting through her mind.

Becky scrambled down the ladder and ran toward the house. While Rachel walked with Matt, a refreshing coolness washed over her in the shade of the old cottonwoods. Running one hand over her hair, she brushed aside strands that had escaped from her braid.

When they reached his pickup, he gazed at her with a serious expression. "If you need anything, just call."

"I will."

Watching him drive away, she wondered if he had any idea how much these decisions confused her. She had to keep the crazy idea of spending time here from taking root in her heart and mind, even though Matt's persuasive words made that task difficult. He loved it here. There was little chance he would understand her eagerness to get rid of the farm where she'd grown up and little chance he could understand her lack of faith.

Chapter Four

Matt tossed a pen on the desk and leaned back in his chair. Releasing a heavy sigh, he looked at John, who sat on the edge of the desk. "I agree. The numbers don't look good."

"That's what I figured, but I wanted your opinion, too."

"Probably ought to see about renegotiating this loan."

"What about the money we got for that alfalfa? Isn't that enough to cover the next payment?"

"Almost, but that doesn't leave anything for other expenses." Matt picked up a computer printout and handed it to John. "You were doing okay until you had to buy parts for the big tractor."

John studied the papers. "We aren't short by much. I could sell a few shares of that mutual fund I've got."

"No, absolutely not. That's Erin's college fund. You know your folks set that up for her. You don't touch it."

John shook his head. "This really shouldn't be your problem."

"My name's on the loan, too. We're partners."

"I know, and I'm grateful for your partnership, but this isn't your livelihood. I hate for this farm to be a burden to you."

"It's not a burden. You know how I feel about the farm. Even though I don't live off the land, farming's in my blood." Matt clapped John on the back. "We'll work this out."

"Too bad this isn't the fall. We'd have a little extra from Sarah's substitute teaching."

"Even that's your family money. Not the farm's. We always agreed that money made outside the farm wouldn't be mingled. If that goes for my teaching income, it goes for Sarah's, too."

"But it could help tide us over."

"Well, it's not the fall, and we have to do something."

"Yeah, I know, but how often will they let us change the terms on the loan?" John set the papers back on the desk.

"We've got a good crop coming."

"Yeah, another great harvest unless something lousy happens."

Without a comment, Matt walked over to the window and looked out on the front porch. Seeing the swing, he thought of Rachel. Just yesterday he was extolling the virtues of farming to her. He pinched the bridge of his nose. He did love this work, but she was right. Sometimes, the uncertainty was painful.

Matt turned back to John. "The corn prices should be better. We'll talk with the bank next week. They'd rather get their money in smaller amounts over a longer period of time than see us default on this loan."

"You're probably right, but I hate to go begging every few months."

"We're not begging. They know we're good for the money. It'll just take longer than expected to pay it back." Matt shook his head. "I refuse to see this farm fail."

Matt followed John out of the bank. "Well, mission accomplished."

John grinned. "Yeah. It's a great feeling to know the financial status of the farm will be good for the foreseeable future."

"Got time for lunch?"

"Can't." John moseyed down the sidewalk toward his pickup. "I promised Sarah I'd get right home, but there's someone you can have lunch with." John nodded his head toward the other side of the street.

Squinting against the sun, Matt glanced in that direction. His heart skipped a beat when he saw Rachel standing in front of the lawyer's office. He looked back at John. "I doubt she's interested in having lunch with me."

"I think you should take a chance and find out."

"Why?"

"Because it's not every day you can have lunch with a celebrity, and you can't deny a personal interest in said celebrity."

Matt smiled wryly. "Yeah. Me and ten thousand other guys."

"Yeah, but the ten thousand other guys aren't here to ask her to lunch." John clapped Matt on the back. "Now get going."

Matt squared his shoulders and stepped off the curb, but before he could say anything, she ducked into the pharmacy. He turned back to John. "Looks like she's busy."

"Not for long. She'll be out in a minute, and you'll be there waiting for her. No more excuses."

"Okay. No excuses." Crossing the street, Matt hoped he wasn't making a big mistake.

Since Rachel's return, he couldn't deny his attraction to her, even though they hadn't seen each other in years. Was there any chance that she could see him in any light beyond friendship? Could she see beyond his scars? Amy hadn't.

What did Rachel think of the quiet, little town she'd left behind for the bright lights of Hollywood? Did the old brick storefronts, uneven sidewalks and potholes in the streets the size of watermelons make her wish she were back in the city? Or did she find something inviting, even charming, about the place she'd known as a child?

He wanted to get to know her again, but he wasn't sure she cared about getting to know him. Why was he even thinking about it? One minute he was telling himself any romantic thoughts about Rachel were ridiculous, and the next he was wondering what he could do to persuade her to stay.

In his heart he knew trying to keep her here would be like trying to keep a beautiful, wild bird in a cage. Even if she fell madly in love with him—a complete fantasy to him—she could never be happy here again.

He had accomplished one mission this morning, why not another one? Letting out a long sigh, he stood in front of the pharmacy, determined to overcome his misgivings.

"Hi, there," he said, shading his eyes against the bright sunshine as Rachel stepped onto the sidewalk. "I suppose you're officially the owner of a prime piece of farm land."

"Yeah. The farm's officially mine." She pushed a stray strand of dark hair behind her ear in a familiar gesture.

He tried to assess her mood without success. "I was on my way to Cramer's Cafe. How about having lunch with me so we can celebrate your new status?"

"I didn't know you had time to while away the hours in the cafe. I thought you helped John in the fields from sunup to sundown in the summer."

"I do, but this is part of the job. I came to town to make a payment at the bank," he said, aware that he wasn't telling the whole story. What would she think if she knew? "And I have to stop in at the cafe to catch up on the local news and gossip."

"I'm not sure I want to celebrate my new status or find out the latest news and gossip."

"Sure you do."

"Do you always insist your invitations be accepted?"

"Only when they're with a beautiful, famous actress who just happens to be my favorite neighbor."

"Maybe I have other plans."

"Do you?"

"No," she replied with a disconcerted smile. "But I'll come only if you promise not to mention a single word about my selling the farm."

"You drive a hard bargain. How did you know I was going to ply you with all the reasons I could think of for not selling?"

"I'm a mind reader."

Matt whistled, then laughed. What would she do if she could read his mind and know how much he'd like to kiss her right here on Main Street? "I'll be careful about what I'm thinking."

Times like these made him want to throw caution to the wind and pursue her with everything in his power, convince her to stay and never leave. However, wisdom dictated that a man didn't throw himself headlong in front of a speeding freight train, and Rachel's determination to be gone was that train. He ushered her into the cafe with that thought firmly in mind.

The smell of coffee and fried food permeated the air as he escorted Rachel to a booth with bright red seats near the door. Several men eating at the counter turned and greeted them. He nodded in return, and Rachel smiled.

"Isn't being with me going to inhibit your chances for hearing the latest gossip?" Rachel asked after the waitress took their order.

"Maybe, but I bet we'll be the main topic. I can hear it now. 'Did you know that Matt Dalton was seen in town today with Rachel Carr?'" He grinned. "We'll be the talk of the town."

"You mean I can't escape gossip even here?"

"I'm afraid not. The local grapevine is as good as the tabloids in these parts. Isn't that one of the reasons you stayed away so long?"

"Yes. The whole town knows everyone else's secrets."

"I like to think it shows people care. You can't live in a

vacuum." Matt wished he could make her realize how much everyone around here cared, but maybe to her, they were just interfering in her life. Did she feel as though people only wanted to get close to her because she was famous? He wanted to ask, but he was afraid she would think him no better than the local gossips.

"Sometimes I wish I could." Sadness emanated from her eyes.

Matt wished he could take away the hurt from her life. The Lord could help if she would only open up her heart. He prayed she would stay around long enough to receive it. "When do you plan to go back to California?"

"Eager to be rid of me?" Her eyebrows puckered in a little frown.

"No." His gaze held hers. Here he was again wishing she would stay forever. If he couldn't have forever, maybe he could have a little piece of forever. "I was going to try to change your mind about leaving, but you made me promise not to mention you know what."

Rachel glanced out the window at the passing pickup trucks and pedestrians before returning her gaze to him. "I don't want to feel guilty for selling the farm."

"Are you feeling guilty?"

"I don't know what I'm feeling. Maybe a little numb."

Matt reached over and placed his hand on hers as the waitress brought their burgers. "That's why I said to give yourself some time. Don't rush into something you may regret later. I know I promised not to mention the farm, but I can't help it."

"That's okay. Your advice is important to me. And you're right—I need to give myself time to weigh my options."

"So does that mean you're staying?"

"I'm still not sure about keeping the farm, but I think you've convinced me to stay at least through the summer."

"That's terrific!" His heart raced as he thought about having her around. "Hopefully, that'll give you the time you need to make the right decision."

"I suppose, but I don't think I'll change my mind about selling." She took a bite of her burger. "Mmmm. As good as I remembered."

"Another reason for sticking around," he said, wishing he were the reason she had decided to stay. He should put aside his personal hopes, but they were all tied up in helping her regain her faith. That had to be her decision, but he prayed for patience and time to help her realize her need for God.

"Hi, Grandma. Where's Becky?" Rachel asked, coming into the kitchen after her trip to town.

The older woman stepped away from the counter and wiped her hands on her apron. "She's in the den playing an intense game of Crazy Eights with Grandpa."

"I don't suppose I can interrupt."

"You could be taking your life in your hands if you tried to stop this match. Your grandfather's pride is at stake here." Kate chuckled. "Tell me. How did it go? Is everything in order?"

Rachel nodded. "It's all mine. Now I have to decide what to do with it."

"I thought you were planning to sell it."

"Eventually, but not right now." Rachel walked over and gave her grandmother a big hug. "I've decided to stay through the summer, but I have to talk with Becky just to make sure it's okay with her."

Kate raised her eyebrows. "I think she'll approve, but what has brought on this change of heart?"

"Lots of little things." An image of Matt flitted through her brain. "Most of all I need a rest, and this is the perfect place to get it." Feeling like a great weight had been lifted from her shoulders, Rachel hugged her grandmother again.

The older woman shook her head. "I can't get over this, but I'm glad."

"Mom, I beat Grandpa!" Becky came bounding into the kitchen.

"You did? Well, good for you." Rachel glanced up to see her grandfather standing in the doorway. "Sorry about that, Grandpa. Better luck next time."

"I don't imagine there'll be too many next times." Shaking his head, Grandpa peered at Rachel. "I suppose you'll be heading out now that the will is settled."

"No, Grandpa, I'm going to stay for a while if it's okay with Becky.

"What do you think, kiddo? Would you like to live here for the summer? In a few weeks the strawberries will be ripe for picking, and we can put them in homemade ice cream. How does that sound?" she asked, hoping to entice her daughter with the good things about the farm—the good things she'd forgotten herself.

"Super!" The little girl eyed her mother curiously, then looked concerned. "Can I bring my stuff from home?"

Rachel put her arm around Becky and hugged the little girl to her. Squatting down, Rachel looked her daughter directly in the eye. "I'll make a few phone calls and have whatever we need shipped out here. We'll have a good time this summer."

Becky gave her mother an impish grin. "Now I can get one of those kittens."

"Yes," Rachel said as she stood. "We'll be here long enough for you to have a kitten."

"Promise?"

"Promise."

* * *

Matt tossed his mail on the table. Before he opened the first envelope, a loud knock sounded on the door behind him. Turning, he saw Sarah through the window in the door. She wasn't smiling. Was something wrong?

"The door's open." He motioned for her to come in.

Sarah bustled into the kitchen. "What's wrong with your answering machine? Do you ever carry your cell phone?"

"Whoa. One question at a time. Answering machine's broken, and I haven't bothered to get a new one. I don't bother much with my cell phone. Can't get a signal half the time. Why?"

"Wade's been trying to get a hold of you."

Concern knotting his stomach, Matt stared at Sarah. "Is something wrong with Wade? Is his cancer back?"

"No—"

"That's a relief. So what's the problem?"

"You haven't responded to Wade and Cassie's wedding invitation."

"That's all?"

"That's all? How can you say that?" Sarah threw her hands in the air. "The wedding's only three weeks away. They need a count for the reception. Wade was worried when you didn't respond."

"I'd never miss my little brother's wedding. We just talked last week. He knows I'm coming."

"Well, the bride gets nervous when you don't send in the response card. Where is it?"

Matt thought for a moment, then headed toward the little room off the kitchen. "Probably on my desk."

Sarah followed. "Well, I hope you haven't lost it."

"Does it really matter?" Matt asked while he rummaged through a stack of papers. "I can always tell them I'm coming."

"Then call Wade right now."

"Man, Sarah, if I didn't know better, I'd think this was your wedding."

"Well, this stuff is important."

Matt held up a little white card and envelope. "Here it is."

"Good. Let's get this in the mail."

"If you say so." Matt chuckled as he handed them to her.

Sarah glanced at the card, then back at Matt. "You didn't put down how many are attending."

"One. Isn't that obvious?"

"The invitation says, 'and guest'."

"And who would be my guest?"

"Rachel."

Matt looked at Sarah, sure his mouth must be hanging open. "Rachel? You're joking, right? She's headed back to California as soon as she can. Besides, what makes you think Rachel would even consider going to the wedding with me?"

"She'll go because you invite her."

"Why would she want to go with me?"

"Because she's known Wade since you were kids."

Matt narrowed his gaze. "Sarah, are you forgetting that Rachel's a big TV star?"

"Are you forgetting that she's your friend? Besides, John told me that you and Rachel had lunch together today."

Shaking his head, Matt laughed. "The local grapevine was one of the things we talked about at lunch. Seems as though it's alive and well."

Sarah gave Matt a perturbed look. "John's not the local grapevine. I'm serious."

"Think about it, Sarah. How could we go together? I've already made my plane reservations."

"She could get on the same flight."

"I'm not so sure at this late date."

"If you don't ask her, I will."

"I can do my own asking."

Chapter Five

Rachel gazed at the prairie sunset while she sat with Sarah on her screened porch. "Becky's having the time of her life catching fireflies with Erin."

"I'm so glad you decided to stay. Erin's found a soul mate in Becky."

"Yes," Rachel replied, thinking about how Sarah fit that role in her own life. Then there was Matt. His presence befuddled her emotions at every turn. Thankfully, she'd seen him very little since her decision to spend her summer on the farm. He worked from sunrise to sundown, leaving little chance for socializing.

Focusing her thoughts in another direction, she said, "I appreciate your watching Becky while I've been taking care of my mother's things. Your support means a lot."

"I'm glad I could help. Besides, Erin loves playing with Becky."

Rachel peered at Sarah in the gathering darkness. "I wish there was some way I could repay you."

"There's no need. What are friends for?" Sarah patted Rachel's arm.

"Thanks for being my friend."

"I should thank you." Sarah chuckled. "Actually there's one thing I'd like. A figure like yours. I've been on so many diets I've lost count."

Rachel smiled wryly. "You wouldn't believe how I hated being skinny all my life. I dreamed of being a petite, voluptuous blonde with blue eyes."

"Surely you wouldn't wish that now," Sarah said.

Rachel chuckled and stretched out her long legs. "You're right, but the old saying's true. 'Beauty's only skin deep.'" Rachel met Sarah's gaze. "You say you envy me for my figure, but I envy you for the way your husband looks at you."

"What are you talking about?" Sarah asked.

"Sometimes, when you aren't paying attention, I've seen John look at you with such love and adoration. I'd like a man to look at me like that." Rachel stared at her sandaled feet.

"I'm sure you get all kinds of admiring looks."

Rachel shook her head. "That's not what I'm talking about. I'm talking about the kind of look a man gives the woman he loves and wouldn't trade for any other woman in the world no matter how beautiful. You're really lucky to have such an adoring husband. That's something I've never had."

"What about Becky's father, or shouldn't I ask?"

Even in the dim light, Rachel could read the curiosity in Sarah's eyes, but she didn't want to talk about Dean. She wished now she hadn't opened her mouth. How was she going to get out of explaining? Rachel tried to smile. "Let's just say that Dean was more interested in himself than he was in me and leave it at that."

"Okay," Sarah said as the headlights of two tractors pierced the dusk and diverted her attention. "It looks like Matt and John are finished for the evening. I have a snack prepared for them when they get in. Would you and Becky like to stay and have some?"

"I really don't want anything to eat, but I'd like to stay and get some advice from John and Matt about buying a horse for Becky. Her birthday's coming up in a few days. She talks horses all of the time." Rachel watched as the tractors pulled into the drive. "Do Matt and John work these long hours all summer?"

"Pretty much."

"I remember Dad working long hours, but not after dark."

"You know the expression. 'Make hay while the sun shines.' Nowadays with their fancy tractors, they can do it in the dark." Sarah laughed. "When it comes to horses, Matt's the one to talk to."

"When I was a little girl about Becky's age, Matt was my hero. I thought he couldn't do anything wrong."

"Did he know that?"

"Never. It was my secret. Why?"

"Sometimes I think he's trying to live up to that image. He tries too hard to never make a mistake. So if you ask him to find you some horses, he'll find the best." Sarah stood and called the girls.

Rachel joined Sarah as the girls bounded up to the house and raced inside. "I'll ask Matt about it tonight if I get a chance."

In the kitchen, Rachel watched Sarah get plates from the cupboard and set them on the counter. Then she cut a cherry pie into eight neat slices.

"Sarah, you know you could lose weight if you didn't have a snack with the men." Rachel held her breath as she waited for Sarah's response.

She glanced up from putting the food on plates. "I'm sure you're right, but I don't have the willpower to resist all this food, especially when I'm serving it. I want to enjoy it, too."

"I'm sorry if you think I'm meddling by saying that."

Sarah turned to Rachel. "No need to be sorry. After all, I

was the one who brought up my weight. My real problem is I don't believe I can ever be thin." Laughing, she added, "I have a fat attitude."

"Would you like me to help you think thin?"

"When do we start?" Sarah asked.

"We can start an exercise program—"

"Oh, no," Sarah interrupted, "I can't stand to exercise. It's so boring, and I'd never stick with it."

"It won't be boring if you have someone to do it with. I have a routine that I use to keep in shape, and we can do it together. It could also be as simple as walking like Becky and I did when we came over this afternoon."

"I don't know." Sarah looked unconvinced. "You'd probably be wasting your time."

"It's up to you, but I'd really like to help if you'd let me." Rachel laid a hand on Sarah's arm. "Dealing with my mother's death hasn't been easy, but your friendship's been wonderful. You've been there when I've needed someone to talk to. Let me help you like you've helped me."

"Okay, I'll try, but don't be surprised if it doesn't work."

"Tell me something, Sarah. Do you pray for me?"

Sarah placed a fork on a plate, then looked at Rachel. "Yes, all of us at church pray you'll let Jesus back into your life. Why?"

"Since I've been back, people keep telling me prayer brings results. If you think praying to God can help me, then why can't it help you?" Rachel leaned back against the kitchen counter and stared at Sarah.

"I never thought of it that way." Sarah shrugged. "You have a valid point, but I'm going to challenge you. If I agree to your plan, you have to attend church with us on Sundays."

Rachel hadn't anticipated this request. She smiled wryly. "You've got me now, don't you? Okay, it's a deal."

"What's a deal?"

Rachel's heart skipped a beat when she heard a familiar male voice behind her. Rachel and Sarah glanced at one another and then back at Matt and John.

"That's our little secret. Right, Rachel?" Sarah said as her gaze slid back to meet Rachel's.

"Sarah's right." Rachel carried plates to the kitchen table.

"Oh, come on, Rachel. You can tell us." Matt pulled out a chair.

"No, this is between Sarah and me. Sorry." Shrugging, Rachel grinned impishly.

"Okay, if that's the way you want it." Matt started eating his pie.

As Matt and John and the girls ate their pie and ice cream, Rachel and Sarah slipped out of the kitchen. They headed for the screened-in front porch where they sat in the old oak rockers.

"You won't tell anyone about my trying to lose weight, will you?" Sarah looked closely at Rachel in the dim light.

"No, not if you don't want me to."

"I don't want people to know I'm trying again, just in case I don't make any progress," Sarah said.

"You have to have a more positive attitude."

"I know, but it's so hard."

"Aren't Christians supposed to be able to do anything with Jesus' help?"

Sarah nodded. "That's the way it's supposed to work, but I guess I've been trying to rely on my own strength instead of relying on Jesus." Sarah sighed. "I'm supposed to be helping you with Christian principles. Instead, you're helping me."

"Well, I remember most of the lessons I learned in Sunday school when I was a kid."

"That seems to be the shame of it all." Sarah gazed at

Rachel. "You know the scriptures, but you've tossed them aside."

Before Rachel could respond, Matt, John, Becky, and Erin joined the two women on the porch. Rachel tried to calm the butterfly feelings in her midsection when Matt stood next to her chair.

Matt looked down at her. "Are you ladies discussing your little secret?"

"Maybe." Rachel grinned at Sarah.

Matt sat on the porch swing. "Any chance of learning about your secret?"

"No," Rachel answered as a distant flash of lightning lit up the horizon.

"Looks like we finished just in time," John said. "The forecast for rain appears to be on the money."

"If that lightning is any indication, you're probably right." Sarah got up and headed for the door. "Let's go in before it rains."

Becky jumped from Rachel's lap and followed Erin, who went into the house behind her parents. When Matt stood to follow, Rachel laid a hand on his arm. He turned to look at her, and her heart caught in her throat as their gazes met. Another flash of lightning illuminated his face, revealing his puzzled expression and the scars that reminded her of everything he'd suffered. "I…I need to talk with you while Becky's not around."

"About what?"

"Sarah said you could help me pick out a horse for Becky. I want to get her one for her birthday. I'd like one for myself, too, so we can ride together," Rachel whispered.

"What kind of horses did you have in mind?" Matt asked, his voice equally quiet. "Is this a surprise for Becky?"

Rachel moved toward the end of the porch farthest from the front door. Matt followed. Breathing deeply, she hoped her voice wouldn't betray the way his nearness sent her pulse jerking like the windblown branches in the yard. "Yes. Becky and I are going to Rapid City to visit with my grandparents for a week. We'll be there on her birthday, but I thought it would be a treat for her to get the horse when we come back. Would you have time to find them before then?"

"You want me to purchase horses without you seeing them first?" Matt leaned against the wall at the back of the porch. "What if you don't like them?"

"I don't know anything about buying horses. My seeing them would make no difference." Rachel looked into the blackness and hoped that not looking directly at Matt would calm her racing heart.

"I think I can help. I have a friend who lives in the Black Hills near Belle Fourche. He supplies stock for the Black Hills Roundup." Matt touched her on the shoulder. "When were you taking your trip?"

Turning to face him, she recognized the futility of controlling her emotions when he was near. "Next week."

He rubbed his chin. "School's out now. I could go with you and take a look at Doug's horses."

"I don't want you to go to a lot of trouble, especially if it takes you away from your work."

"Hey, don't rain on my parade. Don't take away my excuse to have a little time off."

Leaves rustled in the raindrops. Rachel glanced toward the yard as the rain pelted the screens and sprayed water into the porch. "Speaking of rain…"

"Yeah," Matt said, sounding preoccupied.

Rachel waited for some other comment from Matt, but when none came, she spoke hesitantly. "I'm planning to stay a week and show Becky the sights in the Hills. Can you take that much time off?"

"No. John needs my help." Matt stepped closer to Rachel. "But I'll talk with him, then you and I can make some plans."

A sudden gust of wind rattled the screen door. A jagged knife of light split the darkened sky, followed immediately by a booming crack of thunder. Rachel let out a startled cry as she jumped back toward the house. Matt's strong hands held her steady as another flash of lightning skittered across the sky. Again the thunder boomed, and the rain came down in torrents.

"Are you okay?" he asked.

"Yeah," Rachel said sheepishly. "That thunder just caught me off guard."

Matt loosened his hold on her shoulders but didn't take his hands away. Thunder sounded again in the distance. For a moment, Rachel believed Matt was going to kiss her.

"Let's go inside." He dropped his hands and opened the door. "This porch isn't much protection from the blowing rain."

Following him, Rachel wondered about the look she'd seen in his eyes. She was sure he'd wanted to kiss her. So why hadn't he? Did he still see her as only a friend, or at worst, that tag-along kid? Maybe she'd imagined it all.

Rachel glanced at the clock. "I didn't realize it was so late." Then she spied Becky sitting on the couch with her head lying on the arm. "I've got to get Becky to bed."

"I can take you home," Matt said. "John's pickup is right outside the door. If we make a dash for it, we won't get too wet. Umbrellas are in short supply around here."

After thanking Sarah, Rachel hurried across the wet grass with Becky in tow and hopped into the pickup. She pushed back the damp hair the wind had whipped into her face.

Matt joined them as he ran a hand over his face and hair to rub off the rain. He turned the key in the ignition, and the engine roared to life. His strong hands gripped the wheel.

The headlights illuminated the rain-soaked drive. No one

spoke while Matt drove the pickup toward the main road. Sloshing back and forth, the windshield wipers could barely keep up with the rain. A flash of lightning jumped from the clouds and momentarily lit the darkness to near daylight. When another flash of lightning brightened the road ahead, the wide-open spaces of the prairie gave Rachel a feeling of vulnerability.

Slowing the pickup, he turned into the drive leading to her house. When he stopped in front of the garage, the headlights beamed back in the row of windows across the garage door.

Rachel glanced at Becky in the backseat of the extended cab. "She's asleep."

Matt shifted to look. "I can carry her into the house for you."

"Thanks. I'll run ahead and open the doors." Rachel sprinted to the garage. From inside the doorway, she watched Matt slide from the cab with Becky in his arms. Pushing the door closed with his shoulder, he bent forward to protect her from the downpour.

Turning on lights as she went, Rachel led Matt to Becky's room. He deposited her on the bed. Straightening, he turned. "She's still asleep."

"Thanks for bringing us home," she whispered.

"No problem." His golden hair, plastered to his forehead by the rain, appeared darker in the dim light.

His wet shirt, clinging to his broad shoulders and chest, made her more aware of his athletic build. She pushed the thought from her mind. "I'm going to take off Becky's wet clothes. You look pretty wet yourself. There's a towel in the linen closet in the hall if you'd like to dry off."

"Thanks. Do you need one for Becky?"

"No, you took most of the rain." After Matt left the room, Rachel slipped off Becky's damp clothing and put on her pajamas before tucking her into bed. When Rachel stepped into the hall, she bumped into Matt, who was coming out of the bathroom across from Becky's room. She let out a startled gasp.

"Sorry, I didn't mean to scare you. I hung the towel in the bathroom."

"You didn't exactly scare me, but your hairdo is a little wild." She chuckled at the way his towel dried hair stood on end. She longed to comb it back into place. Trying to put some distance between them, she hurried past him into the den. "Are you always so neat, or do you want to impress me by hanging up your towel?"

"How can I impress a famous actress without a comb?" He tried to finger-comb his hair.

Rachel gazed at him, still thinking how tempting it would be to help him. Everything about Matt invited her attention—his strength of character, his infectious laugh, and his mere presence in the room. Against her better judgment she asked, "Would you like to stay until the rain lets up?"

Matt stood looking out the sliding glass door. He slowly nodded his head. "Sure. We can make plans for getting those horses. Let me give John a call and see what he thinks."

"You can use the phone next to the couch while I take Becky's clothes to the laundry room."

When she returned, Matt was hanging up. "John said he wouldn't miss me for a few days. He had a good idea, too. He said we should pull a double horse trailer out to Rapid, then I could drive back with the horses. You and Becky can fly back to Sioux Falls, and we'll drive to the airport there to pick you up. How does that sound?"

"That'll work," Rachel said, wondering how she would survive spending that much time with Matt. He was a temptation that was becoming increasingly harder to resist. "If we leave on Monday, would that work out with your schedule?"

"Yeah. I'll call and tell Doug what you're looking for."

"Why don't you give him a call from here?"

"Thanks, I'll do that."

After Matt made the phone call, he looked at Rachel. "Now that we have things arranged, I'd better head home."

"I appreciate the ride home," Rachel said, still not wanting him to leave.

"It was no trouble." Matt walked through the kitchen, and Rachel followed him.

"Good night," she called after him as he raced through the rain to the pickup. Waiting at the door, she heard the engine turn over. The windshield wipers burst into action, and the headlights punctured the streaming rain with beams of light. She watched him drive away until there was no sign of the pickup.

With a sigh, she headed for the den where she sank down on the sofa. Reaching for the remote control, she turned on the TV just to have some noise and maybe take her mind off Matt. Local news from a Sioux Falls television station blared on the screen.

Rachel stared blankly at the set, but she didn't hear what the newscaster was saying. She could only think of Matt. Her heart ached when she considered the things he'd endured, and yet he always seemed so cheerful. Was it his faith that made him so strong?

Rachel reminded herself that she was a grown woman with a lifetime of experiences behind her. The dreams and ambitions of a little girl had been realized, except one. She'd wanted to share life with Matt. Now the chance to fulfill that dream was possibly within her grasp, but did she dare to reach out and take it?

Chapter Six

"Does everything look about the same as you remembered it?" Matt asked as he drove his pickup down Interstate 90 toward Rapid City.

"Yeah, except I don't remember so little traffic," Rachel said as they passed mile after mile of farmland. "It's so unlike Southern California with cars, cars and more cars. I don't know why the wide-open spaces keep surprising me. Ten years seem to have put a big dent in my memory."

"Do you miss the city?" he asked, hoping she didn't.

"When I have the urge to go shopping."

Matt grinned, trying to hide his disappointment. Her pronouncement didn't surprise him, but it did remind him that her stay here was temporary, and he'd better get that firmly in his mind. "I bet the local five-and-dime isn't exactly what you're used to."

"Not anymore, but I am enjoying the peacefulness of the farm. But I couldn't stay there forever."

"I'm sure you couldn't. Like that old song, 'How can you keep them down on the farm?'" Matt replied, thinking that the smart thing for him to do was forget any romantic notions about Rachel. One day she would sell the farm and go back to her career in California. Would he be a fool to try changing her mind? Even if he did, how could anything exist between them when she still rejected God?

While Matt drove, Becky chattered about the cows, horses, sheep and tractors she saw along the way. She reminded him of the little girl who used to tag along each summer with him and his brothers and cousins. Now that little girl was a beautiful woman and a famous actress, but at the moment she seemed like his longtime friend.

The sun reflected off the hood of his pickup as heat waves radiated from the road ahead. The sky, dotted with clouds, spread out before them like a giant blue umbrella. He tried to concentrate on his driving, but the ease of interstate driving gave Matt ample opportunity to drum up his courage. Sarah had warned him again before he left that if he didn't invite Rachel to the wedding, she would make the invitation for him.

Since he and Rachel had planned this trip, he'd counted the hours until their departure. He wanted to make the most of this time together to renew their friendship, something his long days in the fields had prohibited. But now that he was with her, his fears of not measuring up stood front and center. All of his bravado had evaporated. Thankfully, Rachel's friendly demeanor indicated that she was unaware of his discomfort.

While the pickup hummed along the interstate, Rachel pointed out the Missouri River to Becky as they neared the bridge at Chamberlain. Rachel's beauty shone in everything she did.

How many men would give anything to be in his shoes right now? It would be so easy to fall in love, but he couldn't let himself indulge in the fantasies of a young man. He was physically and emotionally battle-scarred. Besides, he wanted a wife like Sarah, one who loved the life he'd chosen and one who would share his faith. Rachel had grown up and away from the only life he knew. She'd grown beyond his reach.

So why should he ask her to the wedding? A good question—one he couldn't answer.

Matt tried to occupy his mind with driving, but there was little distraction from his thoughts about Rachel in the endless miles of corn and bean fields. Thankfully, Rachel rescued him from his troubled thinking when she suggested they play Twenty Questions, a car game that she'd played as a child. While they played, the landscape changed from neatly blocked farmland into the prairie grasslands of South Dakota's west river country.

When Becky tired of the game, Matt welcomed Rachel's suggestion that they stop at the 1880 Town west of Murdo. They toured the attraction filled with buildings and artifacts that gave an authentic look at life on the South Dakota prairie from 1880 to 1920.

When they returned to the road, Becky pointed out the window. "Look how weird the ground is."

Rachel looked back at Becky. "That's because we're getting close to the Badlands National Park. We'll take a ride through the park. Would you like that?"

"Yeah. This is a cool trip. Did you do this when you were a little girl?" Becky asked.

Rachel nodded. "Many times."

When they entered the park, Becky's curiosity sparked dozens of question as they drove by the eerie but beautiful rock formations. They stopped at the visitor center to pick up information. After they returned to the pickup, Rachel read some of the information to Becky. "Did you know the Badlands was once the floor of a great salt sea and many fossils have been found here?"

"What's a fossil?" Becky asked.

Rachel looked up from the pamphlet in her hand. "Maybe Matt can explain it best since he's the one with the brains around here."

Matt raised his eyebrows. "As I recall, you were never short on brains yourself."

"I just wanted to see if you were awake. You've been so quiet."

"I've been enjoying the scenery," he said, knowing Rachel was the best scenery of all. All day he'd tried to convince himself he was crazy to entertain any notion of a relationship with her other than friendship. But he couldn't ignore this opportunity to see where that friendship might lead. Was he wishing for the impossible? How did God fit into all of this?

"Mom, are you going to tell me about fossils?" Becky asked, shaking Matt from his thoughts.

"Sure. Let's look at this brochure."

Rachel gave an explanation using a picture in one of the pamphlets. The special bond between mother and daughter was evident as they pored over the information. Being with them made him want to share in their rapport. Over the years, he'd observed John and Sarah and longed for a relationship like theirs, but letting dreams of family center on Rachel and Becky would surely set him up for heartbreak. He was a broken man. Why would a famous actress even think twice about a relationship with him?

They continued their drive over the park's scenic route, which took them through the maze of jagged peaks, turrets, spires and canyons of the Badlands. Striae of purples, grays, yellows and reds gave a fairyland effect to the unusual rock formations. Rachel joined Becky in a game, pretending that the spires and turrets were parts of ancient castles or that around the next curve in the road a dinosaur might be lurking. Matt wondered whether the breathtaking vistas made Rachel think about God's part in the wondrous creation.

"Do you want to stop at Wall Drug?" Matt asked as they neared the end of the route through the Badlands. "It's a tourist trap, but it's still fun."

"Yeah. Becky'll enjoy it."

Just a few miles after leaving the park, they drove into the little town of Wall, South Dakota. Soon they were exploring the jumbled collection of shops that comprised Wall Drug and contained everything from junky plastic souvenirs to beautiful art and genuine Native American pottery.

As Becky walked a few feet ahead, inspecting everything in sight, Matt turned to Rachel with a smile. "I know I've said this before, but I can't get over how much she reminds me of you when you were that age."

Rachel laughed. "You remember back that far?"

"My mind's still in good shape." He gave her a wink. "She has that same sparkle about everything."

"I don't remember." Rachel frowned. "All I remember was feeling awkward and uncertain when I was growing up."

"Everyone feels like that sometimes."

"Did you?"

"Sure. I had to follow in Peter's footsteps. He broke all the school's academic and athletic records. That was a tough act to follow."

"You always seemed perfect to me." Rachel stopped for a moment, and her ebony eyes studied him. "I had a crush on you for years."

Her statement punched him in the gut. *Perfect* didn't describe him now. *Damaged* was a better word. He couldn't begin to live up to her childhood image. "I should've known. Right?"

"I was too young for you to notice me then, but I wanted to grow up fast so I could change that." She laughed halfheartedly. "But by the time I grew up, you were engaged."

"And that didn't work out," he said more to himself than to

her. Rachel had cared, but he'd been too blind to see until it was too late. He'd let her slip away like chaff in the strong prairie wind. *But what about now?* He wasn't brave enough to voice the question. Nor had he summoned enough courage to ask her about the wedding. "If I'd only known."

"That I'd be famous?"

"No. That doesn't matter." The unasked question still sat on the tip of his tongue.

Then Becky came tugging at her mother's hand, urging the two adults to see what she'd found. Any chance to voice his question was lost.

After visiting every corner of Wall Drug, they made their way out of town. As Matt drove onto the interstate, Rachel pulled a binder from a canvas bag she had sitting near her feet and began to read.

"What's that?"

She glanced up. "It's the movie script I mentioned."

"Did you get the part?" he asked, wondering if this meant she was leaving sooner than he'd feared.

"Not yet."

"If you don't have the part for sure, why are you studying the script?"

"I want to be prepared if they ask me to read again. I really want this." She fanned the pages with her thumb.

Matt gripped the wheel tighter, steeling himself against what he knew to be true. He'd kept telling himself not to care, all the while hoping Rachel's seeming contentment over the past couple of weeks had meant a change of heart.

"I thought you were enjoying yourself on the farm. It can't be that bad," he added, still hoping to hear her say she was growing to like country life.

"It's been peaceful and relaxing, but I'm not a farmer and never will be." She reached over and touched his arm. "But I'm glad I listened to you and Grandpa about not selling right away. It would've been a mistake to rush into anything."

When she lifted her hand, he felt as if her touch had left a hot brand on his arm. Was she going to brand his heart and walk out of his life again? Why didn't he get the message? She was telling him she had no future on the farm.

"I'm glad you've decided my advice was worth taking." He wondered why he didn't listen to his own advice and forget romantic thoughts of Rachel. "I'd better let you get back to your script."

"Yes. My agent will appreciate it anyway. He thinks I'm perfect for the lead." She sighed heavily. "I've always wanted the lead in a movie."

"I hope you get what you want."

"Me, too."

The next morning Matt walked to his pickup with Rachel and her grandparents. Dew still covered the grass in the shaded areas around the house. The air smelled clean and crisp as the early morning sun peeked through the poplar trees lining the drive.

"I really appreciate your help in getting the horses," Rachel said.

Matt leaned against his pickup. "I wish you were coming with me."

"I don't know anything about horses. Besides, if I go Becky would want to come. And I do want this to be a surprise."

Matt opened the door to the pickup, then turned to George and Kate. "Thanks for letting me spend the night and for the great breakfast."

"Our pleasure," Kate said.

Matt gazed at Rachel. He still hadn't asked her about the wedding. But how was he going to do that with her grandparents standing there listening to the whole conversation? "So I guess I'll see you back home."

She nodded. "You're sure it'll be all right if I don't send any money with you?"

"Yeah, I talked to Doug, and he'll give me a bill." He climbed into the pickup and closed the door. As he rested his arm in the open window, he could already hear Sarah giving him a piece of her mind when she found out he hadn't asked Rachel to the wedding. "Give us a call and let us know when to pick you up in Sioux Falls."

Before he turned the key to start the engine, Becky's small voice sounded from the back of the house. Rachel stepped around the corner and reappeared with Becky skipping alongside, still in her pink nightshirt.

"She's upset because I didn't get her up to see you off."

"I thought you were staying for my birthday." A big pout crossed the little girl's lips.

"I wish I could, Becky." Matt stepped out of the pickup. "I have some business to take care of. Then I have to get back home to help John on the farm. He can't do all that work by himself." Matt bent down and gave her a hug. "We can have a birthday party at my house when you get back home. I know Erin would like that."

Becky's face lit up as she turned to her mother. "Can we, Mom? Please?"

"It's okay with me."

Patting Becky on the head, Matt considered how Becky's appearance had delayed his departure. Was this a sign that he should quit being a chicken and talk to Rachel about the wedding? "We'll plan on it then."

"Great. Then we'll see you at the end of the week." Rachel put a hand to Becky's back and turned to go.

Gripping the pickup's door handle, Matt knew he had to say something now or his chance would be lost. "Rachel, wait."

She turned back. "What?"

"There's one more thing…er…that we need to discuss."

"Okay." Rachel glanced at Becky. "Sweetheart, you'd better go with Grandma and Grandpa, so you can eat your breakfast and get dressed."

"I want to say bye to Matt one more time."

"Okay, one more time, then into the house."

Becky bounded over to Matt and gave him another hug before she hurried off with her great grandparents. Matt smiled as he watched her disappear around the corner of the house. Turning to Rachel, he took a deep breath. This was it. No excuses now.

"Is there something you forgot to tell me about the horses?" she asked.

"No. This is about something else." Matt's heart pounded.

"What?"

"You know I told you about Wade getting married. Well, Sarah thought it'd be a good idea for me to invite you to go to Wade's wedding as my guest. I know it's short notice and all, and you probably can't get a plane ticket at this late date, but if you want to go, I'm sure my family would love to see you. But I know you're probably still busy with your mom's estate. So don't feel like you have to go if you don't want to."

Knitting her eyebrows, Rachel stared at him. Oh man. Had he run off at the mouth like a man with no brain? Oh, yes. Probably worse than that. No wonder she was looking at him as though he'd lost his mind.

"I…I don't know what to say." That little frown still wrinkled her brow.

"Don't worry about it. I understand if you don't want to go." Turning away, Matt opened the door to his pickup.

"I didn't say I didn't want to go. I'm just not sure whether *you* want me to go. Sounds to me as though Sarah pushed you into inviting me, and you're trying to give me every reason in the book to turn you down."

Matt ventured a glance in Rachel's direction. The smile curving her lips made his heart lighter. "That was a pretty sad invitation, wasn't it?"

"Yes."

"Let me try that again. Rachel, would you go to Wade's wedding with me?"

"I'd love to."

"Seriously?"

She laughed. "I said yes, didn't I?"

"You did, but are you sure on such short notice? Can you get a plane ticket?"

"There's one way to find out." Rachel motioned for him to follow her. "We'll use my grandparents' computer."

Matt got out of his pickup. "Your grandparents have a computer?"

"Yeah, I bought one for them a few years ago and insisted that they at least learn how to use e-mail. Now Grandpa can surf the Web with ease."

When they walked into the kitchen, Becky jumped up from the table. "Matt, are you going to stay for my birthday after all?"

Shaking his head, Matt tousled Becky's hair. "Sorry, squirt, your mom and I are going to look something up on the computer."

"Can I help?"

Rachel glanced at the kitchen table where a half-eaten bowl of cereal sat. "No, you haven't finished your breakfast."

"Mom."

"Eat your breakfast." Grabbing her purse from the counter, Rachel ignored Becky's protest as she led Matt down a hallway to a room where a computer sat on a small oak desk. After she turned on the computer, she looked up at him as he stood beside her. "So where's the wedding?"

"Amelia Island, Florida. You'll need to fly into Jacksonville."

"When's your flight?"

Matt shook his head. "Can't remember for sure. I'd have to look at the itinerary I have printed out at home."

"What day's the wedding?"

"The last Saturday in May, whatever day that is. That's all I know." Matt grimaced and pulled his cell phone out of the pocket of his jeans. "I'll call Sarah. She'll find out for me."

Rachel giggled. "She'll be glad to know you've followed her instructions."

"Yeah, tell me about it." Matt punched in the number and in a few moments was talking with Sarah. Then he ended the call. "She's going to call me back after she goes over to my place to get the information."

While they waited for Sarah's call, Rachel searched the Web for details about Amelia Island. "Wow! This is a beautiful place. I've never heard of it before."

"Wade says it's a fairly quiet resort area."

Rachel looked over her shoulder at Matt. "I'd like to take Becky, so she can enjoy the beach, if you don't mind. I'll get a sitter for her while we're at the wedding."

"Sure. She'll enjoy that. Let's hope there are enough seats left on my flight." Matt's cell phone rang, and he flipped it open. "Hi, Sarah. Did you find my flight schedule?"

While Matt relayed the information to Rachel, she quickly pulled up the airline Web site. Her fingers flew over the keyboard as she typed in the dates and times for Matt's flight. "We're in luck. There are seats left on this flight."

"Great." Matt watched her book the tickets and wondered

how he'd let Sarah badger him into this. But the answer was easy—he wanted to spend more time with Rachel. Was he ready?

Rachel set the brightly decorated cake on her grandparents' table in front of Becky. "Okay, make a wish and blow out your candles."

Becky paused for a moment, as if to weigh all her options when it came to picking the best wish. Then with much fanfare she took in a great gulp of air and blew until not a single dancing flame was left. "Yes! I did it. I'm going to get my wish."

"So what did you wish?" Grandpa Hofer asked.

"Grandpa, don't you know you can't tell, or it won't come true?"

"Sorry. I didn't know that rule." He smiled lovingly at his great-granddaughter and gave her a hug. "Since you can't tell me your wish, how about a piece of cake and some of that homemade ice cream?"

"I'm all set to do the honors. The birthday girl goes first, then Grandpa," Rachel said, cutting the cake.

After she served the cake, she sat at the picnic table on the patio where the feast was spread. She ate quietly, wondering whether Matt had found the horses. She missed him more than she believed possible. The realization unsettled her.

Her bad experiences with Dean and her latest boyfriend made her wary of her own judgment. She'd seen them as rescuers in the beginning, but then everything had changed. She was sure Matt wasn't like them. He couldn't be, but what did it matter? She and Matt didn't share the same goals, but she'd accepted his invitation to Wade's wedding. She still didn't know for sure whether the invitation had come because Sarah had pressured him or whether he actually wanted her to go with him.

During the rest of her visit, Rachel took Becky and her grandparents on a picnic at Canyon Lake Park and afterwards visited Dinosaur Park and Storybook Island, where Becky had a grand time looking at the depictions of nursery rhymes and children's storybooks. The next day they went for a drive into the Black Hills to see Mount Rushmore and the Crazy Horse monument. None of these activities did anything to minimize her thoughts about Matt. She was eager to take Becky sightseeing, but she was also eager to get back home.

Home.

With every passing day the farm was beginning to feel like home—the place she belonged.

Chapter Seven

Four days later, as they winged their way across the prairie headed for Sioux Falls, Rachel's anticipation rose with thoughts of seeing Matt. She tried to hide her disappointment when she spied Sarah and Erin waiting for them. Rachel had hoped Matt would come to pick her up, but she should have known after his time off to buy the horses and the upcoming wedding that he'd be too busy.

"Did you have a good trip?" Sarah asked as she approached.

"We had a great time, but it's nice to be back home." There it was again. She was thinking of the farm as home. California seemed far away, and yet, her hopes for a career in films rested there. She was beginning to feel torn between two worlds.

While Sarah drove out of Sioux Falls on Interstate 90, Rachel gazed at the wide-open spaces. For years, she'd hated this prairie, but now it seemed to summon her. The vastness of the sky continued to amaze her. Only an occasional farmhouse or shelterbelt of trees broke the view. The prairie brought her a feeling of peace she hadn't felt in a long time. The very thing that had driven her away seemed to call her back.

Before long Sarah stopped the car in front of the garage. "Here we are. You need some help with your bags?"

"No, thanks." Rachel got out of the car. "I can manage. I appreciate your coming to get us."

"No problem. Erin and I enjoyed the trek to the big city." Sarah smiled. "Matt wants to see you down at the barn."

"We'll put our luggage in the house first," Rachel said, eager to see Matt as well as the horses. "We'll see you later at Matt's."

"Mom, why does Matt want to see us in the barn?"

"He's got something special to show us."

"Is that where my party's going to be?"

"No, he's going to take us over to his house for that." Rachel opened the door to the house, and Becky held it while Rachel carried the suitcases inside. "We have to unpack. Then we can go down to the barn."

"Can't we go down there now? We can unpack later."

"You're right." Rachel grabbed Becky's hand. "Let's find out what's in the barn."

Once outside, Becky let go of her mother's hand and ran ahead.

"Wait for me," Rachel called. "We can go in together."

"Hurry." Becky wriggled with anticipation.

When Rachel reached Becky's side, they went into the barn together. After Rachel's eyes adjusted to the dim light inside, she saw Matt leaning against one of the stalls.

Becky greeted him, then pointed toward the stalls. "Mom, look at the new horses."

Rachel's gaze met Matt's over the top of Becky's head. Seeing him again lifted her spirits. He was someone she could count on. She needed someone like that in her life. Did his invitation to the wedding mean something beyond friendship? She wasn't sure she wanted to know the answer. Becky's tug on her arm brought her back to reality.

"Aren't they beautiful?"

"Yes." Stepping closer, Rachel gave Matt a grateful smile, then looked at her daughter. "I've got a surprise for you. One of the horses is yours."

Becky's eyes opened wide. "Which one?"

"You'll have to ask Matt. He picked them out."

"This little filly right here." Matt pointed to the pony with the black and white pinto coloring.

Becky went quickly to stand beside him. "What's a filly?"

Matt handed her a carrot. "A young female horse."

"So it's a girl horse?" Becky asked as she held out the carrot to the horse, who gobbled it down. "Is Mom's a girl, too?"

Matt nodded. "Yes."

"Can I name my horse?"

"Sure, whatever you'd like," Matt said.

"I think I'll call her Oreo," Becky said. "My dad had a horse named Cookie."

"Hey, Oreo's a good name."

Rachel watched as Matt glanced in her direction after Becky's declaration, but Rachel made no comment. She wondered whether he noticed how the mention of Becky's father made the blood drain from her face. If Matt did, he didn't say anything. He just went about the task of showing Becky how she should feed her horse. Then he took her step-by-step through the grooming process.

There was hero worship in her daughter's eyes as she followed Matt's every move. The little girl wanted a father, and Matt was fulfilling that role. But putting any hope in such a scenario would only bring trouble. Too many differences stood between her and Matt.

"Rachel," Matt said, startling her from her thoughts. "Now it's your turn to meet your new horse." Matt stepped back and Rachel moved closer to the stall. She talked softly as she ran her hand along the chestnut mare's head.

"Mom, are you going to name your horse?"

Rachel glanced down at Becky. "I haven't thought about a name."

"Let me name it."

"Okay, you're good at names."

Becky wrinkled her little brow. "I got it. Sunshine. See how the sun shines on her."

"Okay, Sunshine sounds good to me."

After they finished feeding and grooming the horses, they left the barn.

"Hop in the pickup, and we'll have the rest of the birthday celebration over at my house." Matt opened the door on the passenger side, and Becky scrambled into the back seat of the extended cab.

Rachel followed, fighting off the laughter bubbling inside as she watched her daughter's happiness. She needed to cherish this moment. She wouldn't let thoughts of the past or future crowd out the happiness of today.

When they arrived at Matt's house, Becky barely waited for Rachel to open the door before she slipped out of Matt's pickup. Rachel reached out and grabbed Becky's hand. "Hey, slow down. We have to wait for Matt. After all, it's his house."

"Okay, but let's hurry." Becky grabbed Matt's hand and pulled the two adults toward the house.

When they stepped into Matt's kitchen, John, Sarah and Erin were there to greet them. A beautifully decorated cake and a couple of presents sat on the kitchen table. Everyone sang "Happy Birthday."

After the song, Erin picked up a package wrapped in pink and purple striped paper and shoved it into Becky's eager hands. "Open your presents."

While Becky tore off the wrapping, Rachel went over and stood next to Sarah. "You didn't have to get Becky anything. The party would've been plenty."

"Oh, it's nothing. Just something Erin and I made," Sarah said as Becky opened the box.

Becky pulled out an oval-shaped wooden placard trimmed in wicker that read *Becky's Room*. "Cool. I can put this in my room here, and when we go home, I can put it in my room at home." Suddenly Becky's face clouded with concern. "Mom, what do I do with Oreo when we go back to California?"

"We'll have to decide when the time comes, but don't worry about it now, honey."

"Light the candles, so Becky can make a wish," Erin said.

"Wait a minute." Matt held up a hand. "There's one more little surprise. I'll be right back."

While Matt disappeared down the basement stairs, Rachel contemplated Becky's question. What would she do with these horses when it came time to go? She hadn't wanted to think about the future of the farm. "One day at a time" had been her motto, but she had to make a decision eventually. Maybe she should keep the house, outbuildings, and the land they sat on and sell off the rest. Although the idea had crossed her mind before, she'd shoved it aside every time.

In the beginning, she'd been so determined to get rid of the farm. She had thought keeping even a part of it would mean being disloyal to her father. Those thoughts had been skewed by grief. After all, hadn't her father and mother loved this land? Why had she been so blind to the perfect memorial?

Their farm.

Their granddaughter had opened her eyes. Besides, other Hollywood personalities had second homes, probably in more picturesque and trendy places like Colorado, Wyoming, or Montana.

Before Rachel could settle her mind, Matt returned. He carried a box, which he carefully set on the floor. Immediately, Becky ran to see what Matt had. "Mom, come see. Can I keep them? Please?"

Rachel walked over and looked into the box. Two black kittens mewed and clawed at the side. She couldn't resist picking up one of the small bundles of fur. "Oh, how cute!"

Becky plucked the second one from the box. "Aren't they great, Mom?"

"Yes, they are," Rachel replied, thinking how these kittens were one more thing they would have to deal with when it came time to leave.

Matt touched Becky on the arm. "I've got a bag of kitten food and some kitty litter in the basement. You and Erin take it out to my pickup. Then we'll light those candles and have some cake and ice cream."

Becky and Erin promptly obeyed Matt's request.

"You certainly have a way with kids. I've never seen Becky so eager to get work done," Rachel said.

"They want cake and ice cream." Matt stepped closer to Rachel and put a hand on her shoulder. "I hope I'm not in trouble for giving her the kittens."

Rachel swallowed. How could just a touch make her feel all of the silly things teenage girls felt when they swooned over the latest teen idol? She had to get her act together. She didn't want anyone to guess she was having heart palpitations. "That's okay. Having pets teaches children responsibility."

"You didn't sound so sure for a minute there." Matt wrinkled his brow.

"I was thinking about the things we've accumulated that are going to be a problem when we get ready to leave."

"Don't leave." He didn't glance away until Erin came tugging on his arm. "It's time to light the candles."

When the six candles were burning brightly, Becky stepped closer to the table. "I get two birthday wishes this year. My first wish already came true. I wished for a horse, and I got it. I was going to wish for a kitten next, but I already got that. So now I'm going to wish the best wish of all."

"Why didn't you wish for it the first time?" Rachel asked.

"Because it's hard to get. So I picked easier ones first. Now that I got them, maybe I can get a hard wish."

Curious, Rachel said, "Well, whatever it is, you'd better blow out the candles before they melt all over the cake."

"Okay." Becky took a big breath and grinned in triumph when all the flames went out. "I did it again." Jumping up and down, she clapped her hands. "Now I'll get my wish."

"I certainly hope so." Matt proceeded to cut the cake and put it on plates. "Who wants ice cream with their cake?" When a chorus of *I do's* filled the room, he glanced around. "The birthday girl goes first."

When Sarah took her plate, she cast a guilty look in Rachel's direction. Seeing the expression, Rachel followed Sarah onto the porch where everyone gathered to eat. Matt and John were sitting in the porch swing with Becky and Erin sandwiched between, with their short, little legs dangling. Sarah found a seat on one of the faded green metal chairs at the opposite end of the porch.

Rachel hesitated before she sat down next to her. "Sarah, did you know chairs like this would bring a fancy price in some places?"

Sarah laughed.

"What's so funny?"

Leaning over, Sarah whispered, "I thought you were going to say, 'Sarah, did you know you shouldn't be eating cake and ice cream?'"

Rachel laughed in return. "I'd never say that."

"I'm sorry for accusing you. I was feeling guilty for taking it," Sarah said quietly, looking contrite, but then brightened. "I've been watching what I eat, and I've lost five pounds."

"Hey, that's great." Rachel touched Sarah's arm. "Do you want to start our exercise program?"

"I thought you'd forgotten." Sarah wrinkled her nose. "But I'm glad you're still interested. What do I have to do?"

"We can start on Monday."

"Can't. We're going to my parents' place for Memorial Day."

"Then we'll start Tuesday. Walk over to my place about ten o'clock."

Sarah made a face. "Walk?"

"Yes, that's part of the program—walking. Bring your swimsuit. We can cool off afterwards in the pool."

Sarah groaned. "But I don't own a swimsuit, or at least I don't own one I can get into."

"Then bring along something you don't mind getting wet."

"I hope you know what you're getting into."

"It'll be good for both of us."

Later when Matt drove Rachel and Becky home, Rachel wished their time together wouldn't end. After he helped them get the kittens and their paraphernalia into the house, she stopped him as he started out the door. "Stay and have a glass of lemonade."

"I'd like to, but I have to get back to work. Maybe some other time."

"Thanks a lot for helping us get the horses. I appreciate your help." Rachel and Becky followed him out to his pickup.

"I was glad to do it." He opened the door and slid behind the wheel and placed his arm on the window opening and stuck his head out. "John, Sarah and Erin are going to be gone tomorrow. So I'll be on my own. I could pick you up for church in the morning. Then we can take the horses out for a ride and have a picnic lunch afterwards?"

Rachel wondered whether Matt just wanted to get her to

church or whether the invitation held a more personal interest. Either way her heart soared at the prospect of spending the afternoon with him. But before she could express her own delight in his invitation, Becky jumped up and down, pulling on her mother's arm. "Can we, Mom?"

Rachel's face broke into a grin at Becky's eagerness. "Yes."

Sunlight spilled through the window over the kitchen sink as Rachel finished putting the breakfast dishes in the dishwasher. Matt would arrive any moment. Anticipation sent a nervous tingle down her spine. The thrill of being with Matt played alongside the dread of attending church again.

"Mom, I see Matt's pickup," Becky called over her shoulder as she raced through the kitchen to the back door.

Rachel hurriedly wiped off the counters and dried her hands on a nearby towel. When she turned around, Becky had already opened the door for Matt. Smiling, he stepped into the kitchen.

Rachel's heart skipped a beat as their gazes met. Taking a deep breath, she smoothed her linen skirt. "Hi. I'm surprised Becky didn't bowl you over when she rushed out to meet you."

Matt laughed, and Rachel drank in the sound. His joy over Becky's eagerness touched Rachel deep inside. He'd been through so much, and yet he never complained. Was his contentment a result of his faith? Could she find the same peace? The familiar questions popped into her mind, but her doubts swept them away.

Matt winked at Becky. "You look nice in that pretty blue dress."

Becky smiled from ear to ear. "Thanks. I'm ready to go."

"Okay, we're off," Matt said as he took Becky's hand and went out the door.

Becky skipped alongside Matt whose uneven gait didn't slow him down. With a sigh, Rachel followed after them. She wasn't the only one who was finding it difficult not to care for this man.

During the church service, Rachel's mind centered on the coming events of the day rather than the sermon. She was eager to escape from thoughts about God and her relatives, but after the service was over, she had to stop and talk to every aunt and uncle with a few cousins thrown in for good measure.

When she finally joined Matt and Becky in the pickup, it was a welcome relief. "I thought we'd never get away. I have too many relatives here."

Becky nodded. "Mom, you do have a lot of aunts and uncles."

"I know, and they all want to make sure we're doing okay. Now I'm ready to go on that picnic." Rachel smiled and patted Becky's hand.

"Me, too. I can hardly wait to ride the horses." Becky bounced up and down on the seat. "Let's go."

When they got to Rachel's place, the threesome changed clothes and hurried to the barn. The familiar smell of hay, animals and leather swirled through the warm spring air as Rachel saddled her horse, then watched Matt help Becky put the saddle on hers. He spent several minutes giving the little girl instructions on using the reins to guide her horse. Then he helped her into the saddle and adjusted the stirrups.

He gave the reins the right slack and placed them in Becky's right hand. "Hold the reins here in front of the horn and put your other hand on your thigh like this, while I lead you around the corral. Okay?"

Becky nodded, although her smile appeared uncertain. Her little knuckles were white as she gripped the saddle horn. "You'll stay beside me?"

"Yeah, I'll be right here." Matt walked next to Becky's horse as she rode.

For a moment, Rachel wanted to snatch Becky off the horse and hold her close, but if she was going to have a horse, she should learn how to ride it. She couldn't have a better teacher than Matt. His natural abilities as an instructor showed in his every action and word. After several trips around the corral, Matt stopped in front of Rachel.

"Mom, I did okay?" A grin replaced Becky's uncertain smile.

"You sure did. Are you ready for a real ride?" Rachel patted Becky's white-knuckled hand.

"Are we still going to go slow?"

Matt mounted his horse and looked over at Rachel. "Sure. We'll take it nice and slow for our first trip."

"Let's go," Rachel said, not sure she was ready at all. Riding next to Matt, Becky looked so small on her horse. Was buying her daughter a horse a wise thing?

Why was she having doubts now? Matt and his friend knew a lot about horses, so surely they had picked the perfect pony for Becky. As the horses plodded across the farmyard, Rachel forced herself to relax. Still her mind buzzed with everything about the farm that made her second-guess her decisions. And that included Matt, as well.

Matt glanced at her over his shoulder. "There's a nice shady spot in the shelterbelt across the road where we can eat our lunch."

"Sounds good." Rachel hoped her nervousness didn't show. Becky couldn't know she was worried.

With a slow gait, the horses headed down the lane toward the blacktop road. Soon they reached a cluster of trees, separating two cornfields where the tiny green plants were pushing their way toward the sun through the rich soil. Turning their horses in the direction Matt indicated, they rode along the edge of the trees until they came to a small clearing. He brought his horse to a halt, dismounted and tied the reins to a nearby elm tree.

Matt helped Becky down and showed her how to tie the reins the same way he had. "What did you think of your first ride?"

Becky hunched her shoulders. "It was a little scary at first. I was up so high, but it was still fun."

Matt hunkered down beside Becky. "You'll have to get your mom to help you practice around the farmyard."

"Giving me work to do?" Rachel grinned as she dismounted.

"Sure. You'll have Becky ready for barrel racing before we know it."

Trying to wipe that image from her mind, Rachel chuckled. "I don't think so."

"Mom, what's barrel racing?"

"It's a rodeo sport where riders race their horses around barrels. It takes lots and lots of practice." Hoping to avoid any more discussions about dangerous stunts, Rachel grabbed the rolled-up blanket from behind her saddle and spread it on the ground. "Let's eat. I'm hungry."

"Got the food right here." Matt set the backpack picnic basket on the blanket and started to bring out the food. Rachel and Becky helped. Taking the last container out of the basket, Matt looked over at Rachel. "Do you mind if we say a prayer?"

Rachel shook her head. "No problem."

Becky tapped Matt on the arm. "I want to say the prayer."

"Sure." Matt held out his hands to Becky and Rachel.

While they joined hands and bowed their heads, Becky said a simple prayer. Rachel tried not to think about her daughter's eagerness to pray—something Rachel found difficult to do. While they feasted on fried chicken, potato salad and baked beans, she continued to turn away thoughts of God. But the warm, sunny day and the breeze that chased the puffy white clouds through the pale blue sky made it hard to deny His existence.

After eating her lunch Becky jumped up from the blanket. "Mom, can I pick some of those flowers over there?"

"Sure, just don't wander too far away."

Becky scampered off as Rachel stretched her legs out on the blanket and leaned back on her hands. She gazed up at the clouds floating across the blue background. She'd shoved away thoughts of God, but now all she could think about was Matt. His proximity had her dreaming of tender kisses and whispered promises.

In an effort to corral her thoughts, she asked the first question that came to mind. "Did you ever try to find animal shapes in the clouds when you were a kid?"

"No. Never did that, but I'm sure you did."

"I loved to find pictures in the clouds." Rachel stopped staring at the sky and looked into his eyes. Her heart fluttered. No leading man had as much effect on her as the man sitting beside her. Yet so much separated them. She forced herself not to think of the past or the future. She needed to think about this moment and this moment only and not worry about what it meant for tomorrow.

Matt grinned, and crinkles fanned out from his golden eyes. "I do remember that you had a fantastic imagination."

"That was me all right. My head full of fantasies."

"Look where those fantasies got you. Hollywood. Becky's a lot like you, and she's got a creative companion in Erin."

"They do have fun together. I'm glad Becky has such a good playmate. Staying here has been good for her."

"Has staying here been good for you, too?"

Rachel didn't speak immediately. Being here was therapeutic in a physical sense, but emotionally it was a roller-coaster ride. First, she'd had to deal with her mother's death. Then she had the ever-present reminder of her feelings for Matt. He drew her like a bird to the berry patch, but like the scarecrow, his faith frightened her away.

Rachel's gaze drifted back to the sky as she contemplated

her answer. Being on the farm gave her the peace she hadn't had in L.A. in a long time. Life was so different here that she sometimes forgot the turmoil she'd left behind. "Yes, it's been a welcome change from the hectic life I was leading before Mom died. I'm just sorry she isn't here to share it with me."

"You really miss her, don't you?"

"Yes. I can't explain the silly little things that make me miss her." Tears welling in her eyes, Rachel looked out over the field in front of them. She made no comment as she tried to control her emotions.

"It's okay if you want to cry." Matt moved closer and put an arm around her shoulders.

She leaned her head on his shoulder and let the warmth of his comforting embrace wash over her. In Matt's arms was where she wanted to be. Blinking back the tears, she lifted her head and looked at him. "Thanks. I'm all right now. I get these moments every once in a while. I'll be fine."

"Let's get Becky." Taking her hand, he stood up, pulling her to her feet.

When she was standing he didn't let go of her hand, but continued to hold it as they walked along the edge of the field. It seemed so right, and yet she didn't dare to think about what it might mean.

Becky emerged from the far end of the shelterbelt with a fist full of flowers. She scampered to where Matt and Rachel stood, still holding hands.

Becky thrust the flowers at her mother. "Aren't they beautiful?"

"Yes, they are." Rachel released Matt's hand and took the bouquet of delicate lavender blooms. "Do you know what kind of flowers these are?"

"No. Are they special?" Becky asked.

"Yes. These are pasqueflowers. They're the state flower of South Dakota. I used to pick them when I was a little girl, too."

"Can we take them home and put them in a vase?"

"Sure. Let's head home."

"Last one to the horses is a rotten egg." Becky squealed with delight as she sprinted ahead.

Despite his limp, Matt followed in long strides, leaving Rachel behind. When he reached his horse, he turned around and smiled. Looking down at Becky, he winked. "Looks like your mom's the rotten egg."

Becky giggled. "Yeah. She's the rotten egg."

"That's okay. I don't mind." Smiling, Rachel mounted her horse. "Just wait, Becky. I'll get you another time."

After Matt helped Becky onto her horse, they rode back. When they arrived at Rachel's house, they led the horses into the barn and took off the saddles.

"Mom, can Matt stay for supper?"

Matt shrugged. "I don't know. I have chores to do at home."

Becky ran over and tugged on Matt's arm. "Please stay. Can't you do that stuff later?"

"No, I have work that can't wait, but if you give my horse a rub down, I can go home, finish my chores, then come back."

"We can do it, can't we, Mom?"

"Sure." Rachel turned to Matt. "Bring a swimsuit with you. We'll probably take a dip in the pool."

As Matt left the barn, Rachel realized having him with them seemed so natural. She could imagine the three of them as a family. She shook herself mentally for such thoughts. She couldn't let these thoughts take root in her mind. Matt loved the country life, but even if that weren't a problem, her lack of faith would keep them apart.

But no matter how many times she told herself that, something deep inside wouldn't let her discard the possibility of a relationship with him.

Chapter Eight

"Mom, Mom, you aren't paying attention to what I'm saying." Becky sat on her bed.

Shaking away thoughts of the time they'd shared with Matt over the holiday weekend, Rachel looked at Becky. "I'm sorry, honey. What did you want?"

"Are you going to listen to my prayers?"

"Yes. Go ahead and say them." Rachel never tried to stifle the habit her mother had started with Becky even though she thought they were useless words. She tried to concentrate on what her daughter was saying, but Rachel's thoughts continued to wander to images of Matt. Then Becky's small voice captured her attention.

"And dear God, please let me have a daddy."

So Becky wanted a father. Lately she'd been asking a lot of questions about Dean. She tried to answer honestly but never encouraged Becky's interest in Dean. She didn't want Becky to let her heart linger on the father she'd never known.

When Becky finished her prayer, she lightly touched her mother's arm. "Are you praying, too, Mom?"

"I was just listening to your prayers," Rachel said quickly, hoping to avoid any further questions about prayers or God or Dean. "Now get into bed."

"Okay." Becky slipped under the covers. "You know what I wish?"

"No, what do you wish?" Rachel hoped this wouldn't be a further discussion about Becky's father.

"I wish Matt could be my dad."

Stunned, Rachel looked into Becky's blue eyes, so much like Dean's. "Is that what you wished for when you blew out your candles on the cake at Matt's house?"

"I can't tell, or it won't come true."

"I think you already did. Besides, honey, that wish can't come true."

"Why?"

Rachel let out a heavy sigh. "It's not possible for Matt to be your dad."

"It is if you married him."

"Becky, Matt isn't going to marry me. He's not in love with me. Do you understand?"

"He could fall in love with you and ask you to marry him. Then we could be together all the time just like today," Becky said. "I saw you and Matt holding hands."

"Yes, that's true, but that doesn't mean he'll love me and want to marry me." Rachel paused. "Why do you wish Matt could be your dad?"

"I want a dad like Erin. It isn't fair that she has a dad and I don't."

"Honey," Rachel said as she hugged Becky. "I know how much you miss having a dad. I miss my dad, too."

"Do you miss mine?" Becky asked, pushing herself from Rachel's embrace.

How could she explain why she didn't miss Dean? She didn't want to destroy her daughter's image of her father.

"Becky," Rachel began slowly, "your dad's been dead for over six years. Time helps you stop missing people. In a few years we won't miss Grandma Lynn as much as we do now."

Becky shook her head. "I won't ever quit missing Grandma."

"I didn't mean we'd quit missing her. I meant the missing doesn't hurt so much after a few years," Rachel said quietly as much to herself as to Becky. "It's time for you to go to sleep. No more talking." Placing a kiss on Becky's cheek, Rachel tucked the covers under her small chin and smoothed her hair back from her face. "Sweet dreams."

Much to Rachel's relief, Becky didn't mention wanting a father the next morning. Around ten o'clock Sarah and Erin came over. The two little girls played while Rachel and Sarah exercised. For an hour they bent and stretched to the beat of a variety of songs. Finally, Rachel switched off the CD player, and she and Sarah collapsed on the floor as they wiped sweat from their brows.

"You're going to kill me before it's all over." Sarah laughed breathlessly.

"It'll get easier each time you do it. You did a great job today." Rachel headed for the kitchen. "Would you like some water?"

Sarah followed. "That would be great. All this jumping around makes me thirsty."

Sitting at the table, they were silent for a few minutes while they sipped their drinks. Shattering the quiet, Becky and Erin raced into the kitchen. Becky dumped a pile of mail on the table without stopping as she led Erin to her room.

"What are you girls doing?" Rachel called after them.

"I'm going to show Erin pictures of my dad," Becky answered as she stuck her head around the door frame before disappearing again.

Rachel sat back in her chair and ran her finger up and down

the cool glass of water. "Becky's become obsessed with the idea of a father. I'm not sure how to deal with it."

Sarah eyed her. "Does Becky remember her father?"

"No. Dean died before Becky was born. Even before I knew I was pregnant."

"I'm sorry," Sarah said. "That must've been terrible. At least you've given Becky some memories."

"I tried to do the best I could under the circumstances. But now Becky's praying she can have a dad like Erin, and she has one picked out."

"I bet I can guess who it is."

"I'm sure you can."

"Becky isn't the only one with that idea. I think you and Matt would make a good couple." Sarah sat back apparently waiting for Rachel's reaction.

Rachel shook her head. "You know it wouldn't work. Our lives are on different courses. He'd never want to marry someone like me. He needs a nice country girl. He wants someone who can share his faith as well as his life."

Sarah waved her hand in the air. "You were once a country girl, and you once shared his faith."

"*Once,* but not anymore." Rachel clasped and unclasped her hands. If only she could open up to Sarah and share the reality of the situation with Dean. Would she understand? She released a heavy sigh. "Sometimes I wish I could have faith like you and Matt."

Sarah reached over and touched Rachel's arm. "You can. Just open your heart to God. He's waiting with open arms."

"Not for me. I don't want to talk about it." At times Rachel believed Sarah was right, but she harbored too much hurt and anger. They held her heart captive.

"If you're not interested in Matt, why'd you accept his invitation to the wedding?"

Rachel laid a hand over her heart. So many reasons floated through her mind. How could she explain to Sarah when she wasn't sure herself? "Because I didn't get the feeling the invitation had anything to do with romance. He was so endearing when he asked. He was giving me every excuse to turn him down, so I wasn't sure he really wanted me to go. It sounded as though you'd badgered him into asking."

Sarah laughed. "I did, but only because I knew he wouldn't do it unless I pressured him." Sarah put a hand on Rachel's arm. "After all he's been through he needs some fun in his life, and I thought—"

"You'd play matchmaker."

"You found me out." Trying to suppress more laughter, Sarah stood and pushed her chair under the table. "I'd better get Erin and head home." Sarah made her way back to the bedroom where the girls were playing. "Okay, Erin, it's time to go. I have lots of work to do at home."

"Mom, can't I stay a little longer? We didn't get to swim."

Sarah shook her head. "We've got to go. We'll be coming over here a lot this summer, so you can swim another day."

Rachel stepped into the room. "I'll watch Erin if she wants to stay."

"Okay, if you don't mind."

"I don't," Rachel said as loud cheers filled the room.

"Seems you've made two little girls very happy." Sarah stepped back into the hallway.

Rachel followed Sarah back to the kitchen. "When do you want me to bring Erin home?"

"When Matt's there so I can do more matchmaking." Sarah grinned.

Putting a hand on one hip, Rachel pursed her lips. "You don't give up, do you?"

"No, because I'd like to see Matt find someone. My heart broke for him when Amy called off their engagement."

Rachel wanted to ask what happened, but she wasn't sure this was the right time. "So what makes you think I'd be any better for him?"

Sarah shrugged. "When you're together, his eyes light up…and so do yours."

"That doesn't mean we suit each other."

"Yeah, but I say it's something to explore. I'm so glad you said you'd go to the wedding with him. He did tell you it's a beach wedding, didn't he?"

Rachel nodded. "And that got me to thinking maybe it isn't such a good idea for me to go."

"Why?"

Rachel glanced at her feet. She didn't want to sound full of herself, but Sarah had no idea what could happen if the paparazzi somehow got wind of this trip. "I wouldn't want to ruin the wedding."

"How could you ruin the wedding?"

Rachel let out a harsh breath. "So far since I've been back here, and even on my trip to Rapid City, I haven't had to deal with fans or reporters. I was almost feeling anonymous again. But I never know when reporters might be lurking, especially on a public beach. I'd hate for them to show up and ruin Wade's special day."

Sarah frowned. "Do you think that could happen?"

"It's always a possibility."

"But not likely, right?"

"Yeah, but I don't want to set up expectations for Becky, for me, or for Matt."

"You'll be leaving in just a couple of days. Go and have fun. What have you got to lose?"

My heart. The phrase flitted through Rachel's mind, but she couldn't let Sarah know. "Nothing I guess."

* * *

The sight of Matt in his navy-blue suit, standing against the backdrop of the dunes and ocean, nearly took Rachel's breath away. He always looked great in the jeans and shirts he wore around the farm, but she wasn't prepared for how devastating he looked in a suit.

"Are you ready?" Matt smiled as he stepped into her rented oceanfront condo.

"Mom, you and Matt match."

Nodding, Rachel ran her fingers down the skirt of her navy silk chiffon dress. "I guess we do."

"I want to match."

Matt hunkered down next to Becky. "You don't have to match, because you look so pretty in your sundress." Matt stood again. "We'd better go. We have to walk across the parking lot to get to the walkover. It's on the other side of the fence."

"I'm ready." Becky headed for the door.

Rachel slipped her arm through Matt's. "Thanks for letting her attend the wedding."

"Don't thank me. Wade and Cassie insisted, especially after Becky bonded with Taylor and Makayla. The three girls are having a ball together."

"I can't get over the change in Becky. She used to be so shy, but now she makes friends with everyone. First Erin and now Cassie's little girls."

"I'd say being on the farm's been very good for her and her mother." Matt glanced at her with a knowing smile. "Wouldn't you say so?"

"I'm not going to argue with you."

"Good."

As Matt led them toward the gate, the sun sat in the western sky just above the tree line, casting long shadows across the parking lot. Although the daytime temperatures had been in the mid-eighties, an afternoon sea breeze had already cooled the air.

Matt opened the gate, and the threesome joined Matt's parents, grandparents and a couple of elderly aunts, who were already waiting on the beach walkover. Gnarled live oaks created a canopy that shaded the weathered wooden planks of the walkover. Greetings, hugs, and lively conversation rippled through the gathering while the fifty plus guests made their way toward the beach.

With Becky clinging to one hand, Rachel ambled along the walkover and down the stairs that led to the beach.

"Mom, I'm getting sand in my sandals. Can I take them off?"

"Sure. I'm going to take mine off, too." Rachel glanced over at Matt. "You go ahead. Wade and Peter are already waiting for you."

Matt smiled. "Sure. I'll see you down there."

The breeze ruffled the hem of her dress around her legs. A strand of hair blew across her face. Pushing the hair behind one ear, she took in the scene before her—family and friends gathered to celebrate Wade and Cassie's love for each other.

How would her life have been different if she'd taken the time to share *her* marriage with family and friends rather than eloping? So many events surrounding this celebration took Rachel back to the mistake she'd made in not including her family in her plans. She shook the thought away. She wouldn't relive the past.

But by coming to the wedding with Matt, was she rushing headlong into another relationship that wouldn't work out? No. She was here as his friend, but did he have other expecta-tions? That was a question she almost didn't want to answer.

While the wedding guests gathered near the arbor, decorated

with flowers, greenery and tulle, a violinist began playing a se-
lection of classical music. The rhythmic sound of ocean waves
spilling onto the sand served as an accompaniment.

Matt stood between Wade and Peter at one side of the arbor
against the backdrop of clear blue sky and ocean. Rachel
couldn't help comparing the brothers. Matt stood taller, his
broad shoulders very evident in that suit. His straw-colored hair
contrasted with his brothers' darker brown. Her heart did one
of those familiar flips as he laughed at something Wade said.

Closing her eyes for a moment, she took a deep breath. She
didn't want to care, but she couldn't deny the feelings that
surfaced every time she was around Matt. He'd always been
the one she noticed, even the first time the three brothers came
to visit their cousins on the Dalton farm. Although scars marred
his face now, he was still handsome in her eyes.

His caring heart had won her from the start. Wade and Peter
were never unkind to her, but Matt always went out of his way
to include the skinny little girl who wanted to fit in with the
boys. She witnessed that same kindness again and again as he
interacted with Becky. Could he be the father Becky longed
for? Rachel stopped herself—she couldn't begin to think like
that.

The violinist started the processional music, and Becky
tugged on Rachel's arm. "Mom, here come those little boys."

"Jack and Danny?"

Becky nodded. "They have rings in those treasure chests.
And I see Taylor and Makayla. They're supposed to throw the
shells in their baskets."

Rachel placed a finger on her lips, then whispered, "We've
got to be quiet now."

Becky nodded and turned her attention back to the proces-
sion. After all the children arrived at the arbor, Wade gave the
two little boys a pat on the head and hugged the little girls.

Becky tapped Rachel's arm and pointed. She looked in that direction.

Cassie appeared at the top of the walkover, her long dark curls covered with a waist-length veil that waved in the breeze. Dressed in his army uniform, Cassie's oldest brother escorted her down the stairs and across the sand toward the arbor. Rachel wondered whether seeing the uniform made Matt think about his time in the service and everything he'd suffered.

Rachel blinked back tears as Wade took Cassie's hands and they stood facing each other. Their faces radiated with happiness—happiness so tangible Rachel felt as though she could reach out and touch it.

Then she glanced at Matt. His gaze met hers, and her heart fluttered. Taking a deep breath, she tried to concentrate on the ceremony, but every word and every vow brought her thoughts back to Matt. She tried to remind herself of the reasons she shouldn't think of him as more than a friend, but they slipped away as easily as the sand slipped through her toes.

During the ceremony Wade and Cassie took a shell from one of the baskets Taylor and Makayla carried and repeated a scripture together. Then the little girls walked through the gathering and held out the baskets so each guest could take a shell and toss it into the ocean as they recited a blessing for the new couple.

After the minister pronounced Wade and Cassie husband and wife, Wade kissed his bride and the guests applauded. Rachel tried not to think about kissing Matt. Would the whole day serve to underscore Sarah's attempt at matchmaking? Rachel was falling victim to that dangerous thinking.

She tried to refocus her thoughts during the recessional, but Matt's smile as he shook Wade's hand and hugged Cassie captured her attention. He was happy that his brother had found someone who loved him. Sarah's words about Matt echoed through her mind. *I'd like to see Matt find someone.*

Why was she here if she didn't want to be *Matt's someone?*
That question continued to haunt her.

While the wedding party stayed at the beach for photos,
Rachel and Becky joined a number of the other guests at
an oceanfront home for the reception. As they opened the
door of the screened porch that surrounded a sparkling pool,
music greeted them along with servers carrying trays of hors
d'oeuvres.

Becky tugged on her arm. "Where are Taylor and Makayla?"

"They had to stay on the beach to get their pictures taken
with the bride and groom. They'll be here soon."

"Is that where Matt is, too?"

Rachel nodded as she viewed the off-white tablecloths and
sea horse centerpieces on the half dozen tables surrounding the
pool. Tonight she was just another guest. She relished the
freedom of obscurity.

"How's the prettiest girl here?" Matt whispered in her ear.

Smiling, she turned. "How'd you sneak up on me?"

"You seemed lost in thought."

"Guess I was," she replied. "Done with the photos?"

He nodded. "At least the ones I was required to be in. Don't
like having my picture taken. Did you and Becky get something to eat?"

"We did."

"Good. I'm going to snag something for myself." Matt
grabbed a stuffed mushroom from a passing server.

Matt's mother, Gloria Dalton, approached, waving a hand as
she motioned to him. "Matt, the photographer wants to take
more pictures of the wedding party in front of the pool fountain."

"More pictures?" Consternation showed on Matt's face.

"Yes, you'll survive." She patted him on the back.

"Little brother owes me big," Matt mumbled as he walked
toward the group gathered near the fountain.

Gloria turned to Rachel. "Ever since his injuries, he's hated to have his picture taken."

Rachel wanted to say she understood his wanting to avoid cameras, but she wasn't sure how her observation would come across. She didn't know what to say to Matt's mother. Until last night at the rehearsal dinner, Rachel hadn't talked to the woman since she was a teenager. Even last night their conversation had been minimal. What did she think about her presence here with Matt?

"I didn't get a chance last night to tell you how sorry I was to hear about your mother." She patted Rachel's arm. "Are you doing okay?"

Rachel nodded. "Most of the time."

"I can't relate to your situation completely, but our family's been through a lot, too. We're just thankful that Matt's doing well now, because he suffered so much."

"And Wade, too. Matt told me about Wade's battle with Hodgkin's disease."

"Then you'll understand if I'm very protective when it comes to my sons."

Rachel wondered where this conversation was headed. "I do."

"Good. I'm going to be very blunt with you. I don't want you to hurt Matt. He's been through enough."

Rachel swallowed a lump in her throat. How could she respond? She glanced across the pool to where Matt laughed with his brothers as the photographer snapped pictures. She had to defend herself. "What makes you think I'd hurt him?"

"Oh, I don't think you intend to hurt him, but I see the way his eyes light up when he looks at you."

Sarah's exact words. "What are you trying to tell me?"

"I'd rather you didn't get involved with him. He's not ready to deal with your celebrity."

Why was she so conflicted? She'd been warning herself not to get involved with Matt, but hearing his mother say that very thing made Rachel want to do the opposite. Did Wade and Cassie's happiness make her want the same for herself?

"We're not involved," Rachel finally replied.

"Well, make sure *he* understands that. He's a quiet man who loves the country. He'd be lost in a big city. That's why he left Atlanta."

Despite Gloria's explanation, hurt stung Rachel's heart. She wondered whether she was only interested in the thing she couldn't have. Surely she wasn't that shallow. Had Hollywood jaded her in some way? Maybe that was what Matt's mother saw.

Before Rachel could make another response, Matt sauntered toward them. "Hey, Mom, are you getting reacquainted with Rachel?"

Gloria smiled. "Yes, we've been having a lovely conversation."

"Did you survive the photo session?" Rachel asked, trying not to think of the conversation that she wouldn't classify as lovely at all.

"Yeah, I survived, and now I understand why you aren't always excited to be on the other end of some photographer's lens." Matt glanced around the pool enclosure, then turned back to Rachel. "Pretty fancy place, but I suppose you're used to stuff like this."

"It's a beautiful place for a reception," Rachel said, hoping to avoid any discussion of her life in California. Then Wade announced that the guests should start through the buffet line, and Rachel welcomed the escape from more conversation with Gloria.

Rachel joined Matt at the table with the bride and groom and their attendants, while Becky sat with the other children at their own special table. Eating dinner and toasting the happy couple passed by in a happy blur, the conversation with Gloria forgotten.

After Wade and Cassie cut the cake, the children took their cake and went with a sitter to one of the nearby condos. Then Cassie tossed her bouquet, and Peter's date caught it. So Wade threw the garter in Peter's direction. Lots of loud laughter, joking and backslapping ensued as Wade's friends made sure Peter got the garter.

Standing off to one side, Rachel smiled at their frivolity while she sipped some punch. When the hubbub subsided, Matt glanced around the area. When he saw her, he smiled and walked her way.

"Enjoying the antics of grown-up boys?" He laughed.

"Yes, you are all quite entertaining."

Matt turned his attention back to Peter and his date. "I bet my mother doesn't consider it entertaining."

"Are they serious?"

Wade chuckled, then leaned closer. "Absolutely not. Besides my mother would probably have a fit if they were."

"Why?" Rachel asked, thinking of her talk with Gloria.

"Mainly she's too young but overall not suitable."

"And your mother told you this?"

"No. She told Peter, and he told me when we were discussing her disapproval of Wade and Cassie's relationship."

Rachel took in the information. Was this Gloria's modus operandi—discourage her sons from any relationship? "So Wade and Cassie ignored her?"

"No, she finally realized her mistake. But she's overzealous to protect her boys because all three of us have been through broken engagements."

"Sounds like she just wants to see you happy," Rachel said, reflecting on Gloria's warning to her.

"Yeah, but eventually she has to realize we're all grown up and can take care of ourselves." Matt chuckled and put an arm around Rachel's shoulder and pulled her close. "We try to humor her."

"I guess that's all you can do."

She wanted so much to ask Matt about his broken engagement, but this was information he would have to volunteer. And he didn't seem inclined to discuss it. While Rachel mulled over the situation, Peter announced that Wade and Cassie were getting ready to leave.

Rachel and Matt followed the other guests to the front of the house where a limousine was parked. Clutching her little bag of rice, Rachel stood next to Matt while they waited for Wade and Cassie to come out. When the newlyweds appeared and rushed to the limousine, the air filled with rice and cheers.

As the limousine drove away, Matt turned to Rachel and chuckled. "You've got rice in your hair."

"I do?" She reached up and touched her hair and brought away a few pieces.

"Here. Let me get it out for you." He gently picked the white stuff from her hair.

His nearness made Rachel's heart flutter. His proximity enticed her to put her arms around him, but she resisted the temptation. Suddenly he stopped and abruptly strode across the lawn to where the photographer was snapping photos. Matt stood right in front of the camera. The photographer looked up at Matt, and an animated discussion followed. Rachel knit her eyebrows in concern.

As abruptly as he left, Matt returned. He took her hand. "Let's go."

Chapter Nine

Trying to figure out what he was going to say, Matt held Rachel's hand and led her across the walkover to the beach. Sea oats, bathed in moonlight, danced in the breeze. The full moon illuminated the wide expanse of packed, wet sand left by the ebb tide.

While Rachel removed her shoes, Matt took off his own shoes and rolled up his pant legs. Then they walked without talking across the sand to the water's edge. Stars twinkled in the clear night sky, making the warm spring night picturesque and peaceful. The waves spilled onto the sand. Their rhythmic sound did nothing to soothe his troubled thoughts.

"Now that we're here, are you going to tell me what was going on back there?" She peered at him in the dim light.

Matt stared back at her and remembered how she'd looked earlier as she held Becky's hand. Beautiful. And she was here with him—the most unlikely man.

What would she say about the photographer? Would she think he was interfering? He sighed and looked out at the water. "You know that photographer?"

"Yeah, what about him?"

"Well, I was watching him for a while tonight. At first, I thought it was my imagination, but eventually I became convinced that he was taking too many photos of you."

"So what did you do?"

"I confronted him, and he admitted he wanted the photos so he could sell them."

"Were you able to convince him not to do that?"

Matt laughed halfheartedly. "No, and I realized there was nothing I could do about it, unless I took his camera. I couldn't do that because Wade and Cassie want the photos of their wedding."

Rachel touched his arm. "Thanks for trying to help, but it comes with the territory. If the guy wants to make a few bucks on the photos, let him."

"So you don't care?" He wondered whether she thought he'd overreacted.

"I care, but I learned a long time ago that there are some battles you can't win. I was more worried that my presence might take away from the wedding. So if the photographer took a few pictures of me, no harm. I'm just glad everything was wonderful for Wade and Cassie. They looked so happy."

"They did, didn't they?" Matt said, thinking how he'd like to have his share of happiness. And against his better judgment, Rachel seemed more and more a part of that thinking. "Would you like to go for a walk?"

"I thought that's why you asked me to come down here, or was it so you could get me alone?"

He laughed. Did he dare hope she wanted to be alone with him? "You found me out."

She joined in his laughter. "So now I know your true motives."

"Maybe I really wanted to find out what you and Sarah are keeping a secret."

She chuckled. "You don't give up, do you?"

"Nope."

"I promised Sarah I wouldn't say anything, and I keep my promises. If she wants to tell you, that's her business."

"You and Sarah have become good friends, haven't you? I was a little surprised, because she was prepared not to like you."

"Yeah. I sensed that, but I was determined to make her like me." Rachel laughed. "I've never had a friend like Sarah."

"Sarah's a good listener. When she gets to know you she can read you like a book." Matt knew that firsthand. Sarah had immediately noticed his interest in Rachel.

The trouble was he didn't know how to deal with that interest. Being around her confused him. He wanted to be her friend, but he wanted so much more. Matt put his arm around Rachel's waist and breathed a sigh of relief when she leaned into him and put her arm around his waist. They wandered down the beach in silence.

Still arm in arm, they stopped for a moment and turned to gaze out at the ocean. Matt stared out at the darkened water, accented by the white of the breakers. "I remember the first time I saw the ocean when I was a kid. The vastness and power fascinated me."

"I never saw any ocean until I moved to California, except amber waves of grain."

"Yeah, I know what you mean. That's pretty much the kind of waves I look at these days." Chuckling, he turned to face her.

"I'm kind of liking those amber waves again. I never thought that possible." Her eyes twinkled in the moonlight.

"So you're finally admitting you like it on the farm."

"Maybe."

"Still can't pin you down?"

"I'm still determined to take one day at a time." She turned and started down the beach again.

"And you should," he said as much to himself as to her.

"You're sounding like my grandpa. He's always agreeing with me, but underlying there's a little bit of disagreement." She laughed and hurried ahead.

Hoping she didn't notice his limp that much, he caught up to her. "Hey, I'm not sure I like being compared to an old man."

Stopping, she turned and smiled at him. "I'm not comparing your ages, but your wisdom."

Was he really all that wise? Right now her nearness was playing havoc with his senses. He wanted to take her in his arms and kiss her, but that would only complicate matters. He'd brought her out here to talk, but the idea of kissing her kept resurfacing.

When he'd invited her to the wedding, he had these grand plans about how he was going to confess his feelings for her, but he'd be a fool to do that. She would go back to California and her career in a few weeks and never return. He didn't want to lay his hopes and feelings on the line and have them dashed.

She never tried to hide the fact that she'd had a crush on him when she was younger, but she made light of it every time she mentioned it. Besides, he wasn't the young man she remembered. He was battle-scarred from combat and love. He wondered what Becky's father had been like. She never talked about him. Did she have scars, too? She'd lost a husband. What was his broken engagement compared to the loss of her husband and the father of her child?

He should forget any romantic notion about her, but like a burr on a pant leg, he couldn't shake it. How much easier it would be if they could go back in time, and she could be plain Rachel Charbonneau, instead of famous Rachel Carr.

Every time he'd wanted to kiss Rachel Charbonneau, Rachel Carr got in the way. But he wasn't going to let it happen again tonight. After all, she was once the young girl who'd shared her dreams with him. This time he would make his dream come true.

He gently took her hand and pulled her close. Putting a hand at the back of her head, he leaned forward. His lips met hers in a warm and tender kiss. He wanted to make her his, but how could a simple schoolteacher win the heart of a famous television beauty? One kiss would never be enough.

When the kiss ended, he said nothing. He gazed at her as he pushed a wisp of hair back from her face. The silence said more than words ever could. These feelings were something he would need more time to explore.

They needed this time together. Then maybe she would see the need for God in her life, if he could set the right example. Would she walk away from him and God?

Rachel gazed into Matt's eyes. His fingers lingered on her cheek after he pushed her hair back from her face. His touch made her stomach churn like the nearby surf. She leaned into him and wrapped her arms around his waist. His arms tightened around her.

They continued to stand in silence. Being with Matt made her heart sing, so she feared saying anything that would break the wonder surrounding them at that moment. She could dream nothing would separate them, but they couldn't erase the world around them. How was she going to deal with her ever-growing feelings for him?

Was she letting herself fall into another emotional disaster? But his kiss made her want to forget his mother's warning, forget her one-day-at-a-time motto, and forget her fear of letting another man into her life. What could she say to him? He hadn't said anything. Maybe he was sorry he'd kissed her. She hoped she hadn't made a mistake in coming to the wedding with him.

When he ended the embrace, he took a step back. His gaze searched her face. "Maybe I shouldn't have kissed you, but you've stirred some long forgotten feelings, and I'm not quite sure what to do with them."

Sighing, Rachel gave him a weak little smile. "I'm glad you kissed me. I think I've wanted you to since forever. But I had to grow up first."

"And now, what should we do about it?"

"I'm not sure. Let's take it one day at a time."

Laughing, Matt draped an arm around her shoulders and pulled her close. "Leave it to the woman who's resisting God to remind me of something in the Bible. 'Do not worry about tomorrow, for tomorrow will worry about itself.'"

"Good advice. Hard to follow." She sighed again.

"Yeah. Let's head back." He held out his hand.

She put her hand in his and fell into step beside him. The warmth and strength of his hand, closed around hers, gave her a sense of security and made her want to disregard her vow to take one day at a time. Tomorrow they'd be back on the farm and facing the reality of their different lives, and this fairytale weekend would be only a memory—a wonderful and fabulous memory. Still, something was happening between them. Was it wise to explore?

The following evening, after their flight back from Florida, Matt stopped his pickup in Rachel's drive. He glanced at her with a puzzled frown. "Do you always leave lights on?"

"Yes, I have a light on a timer. Why?"

"I didn't remember you doing that."

"You probably don't remember because the only time you've been here after dark was the night you brought us home in that thunderstorm. You were concentrating on not getting wet."

"You're right."

"I hate walking into a dark house. A habit from L.A., especially when I lived in the low-rent district." More than that, she hated going into any house alone. Even here on the farm where they'd never locked a door when she was a kid, she couldn't forget her fears.

"Now you probably have a security system."

"How'd you guess?"

"It's something I'd expect a rich, television star to have, but you don't need to worry about having a security system tonight," he whispered, pulling her close. "I'm here. I'll protect you from all the bad guys."

Rachel gazed ahead at the yard light casting long shadows across the ground. Matt had gotten a little taste of the real bad guys in her life when he'd confronted the photographer at the wedding, people like that who invaded her privacy at every opportunity. But what could she expect? Such intrusions were part of the life she'd chosen.

Still the constant hounding often made for an unsettled life. Since she'd come back home, she hadn't been on their radar. On the farm, peace had returned to her life.

"Good," she said, her mind hopscotching from the threat of reporters to the threat of emotional danger Matt represented. Who would protect her heart if she couldn't forget him when it was time to leave? She wanted to put aside her reservations, but the joking comment about the security system underscored the differences she couldn't force from her thoughts. Before she could talk herself out of what she really wanted, Matt's lips claimed hers, and the romance of a moonlit night replaced any gloom.

When the kiss ended, she breathed in deeply. "Let's go in."

He opened the door and with a sweeping motion helped her out of the pickup. "My fair princess, your castle awaits. Where's your key?"

Rachel reached into her purse. "Right here."

Stepping to the back door that led into the kitchen, Matt inserted the key into the lock. Before he turned the key, the door swung open. Chuckling, he turned toward her. "So much for security. Are you sure you locked this?"

Rachel's heart jumped into her throat. Grabbing Matt's arm, she pulled him away and whispered, "Don't go in there."

He frowned. "Why? What's wrong?"

"Did you hear that noise?" Breathing deeply, Rachel gazed at Matt in the dim light. A dog barking in the distance reminded her of how far away they were from the next farm and help. He probably thought she was crazy. "I think there's someone in there."

"I didn't hear anything."

"I did." Rachel's heart hammered. Fear hastened her steps as she dragged him toward the garage entrance. "Come with me."

"You're blowing this out of proportion." He followed her until they stood near the side door that went into the garage. "Let's go inside and look."

"No." Rachel leaned back against the side of the house.

Matt gathered her close. "Tell me what's wrong."

"Someone broke into my house a few weeks before I got word that Mom had died. It was so creepy." Rachel shuddered. "Even the security system didn't help."

"No wonder you're apprehensive." Caressing her hair, Matt continued to hold her. "Let me check things out. You can stay here or go with me. Whatever you want to do."

"Go with you." She didn't want to be left alone in the dark. Too many nights back in L.A. she'd lain awake listening for noises and prowlers that never came. She believed she'd found safety here. Now that peace was shattered, too.

She took Matt's hand and the strength and warmth of his

hand reassured her as they walked into the dark garage. Groping their way, they walked around her new SUV.

As they neared the door going into the house, Matt grabbed the old baseball bat sitting in the corner. Peering at her in the faint light, he whispered, "Just a precaution."

"Be careful." Rachel's heart beat so hard she was sure the sound was echoing off the walls.

They climbed the two steps that went from the garage into the laundry room. Matt carefully opened the door. They went inside. The pale light from the den barely illuminated the kitchen. The refrigerator hummed, the only sound in the quiet house.

Still holding Rachel's hand, Matt crept through the kitchen. Suddenly, he lurched forward while a loud yowl broke the silence. Losing his balance, he fell just inside the den, bringing Rachel down with him. The bat sailed from his hand and landed with a crash against the coffee table.

Rachel lay by his side. "Are you all right? You must've tripped over one of the kittens."

"I'm not sure," he groaned.

She leaned over to examine him. Without warning his arm snaked out and pulled her close. "Lie still. I hear footsteps."

She lay perfectly still. She couldn't breathe. A man appeared, silhouetted in the hallway leading to the bedrooms. Her scalp prickled.

"Rachel, is that you? What's happening out here?" The familiar voice made her sit up.

"Art!" she cried. "Where'd you come from? What are you doing here? You scared us to death."

"I scared you? I think it's the other way around." Art sauntered into the room. "What's all the racket?"

Rachel scrambled to her feet while Matt slowly uncoiled his tall frame to stand beside her.

Matt eyed the stranger. "Who's this?"

"Oh…I'm sorry, Matt. I was so startled I completely forgot you two don't know each other." She glanced from one to the other. "Matt, this is Art Bishop, my agent. Art, this is Matt Dalton, an old friend."

Art glanced at Rachel and then extended his hand to Matt. "I'm glad to meet you, Matt." Art smiled, but there was no warmth in his eyes.

"Thanks. It's nice to meet you, too." Matt put a proprietary arm around her shoulders. "She was a little frightened when we discovered the door was unlocked. How'd you get in?"

"Your friend Sarah let me in."

Frowning, Rachel shook her head. "We were just there to drop Becky off to spend the night with Erin, Sarah's little girl, and she didn't mention seeing you."

Chuckling, Art looked at Rachel. "That's because I told her I wanted to surprise you."

"Well, you're lucky Matt didn't knock you out. Ever since the break-in back in L.A., I've been a little on edge. I thought you were another intruder."

Art rubbed his hand over his face. "I wanted to surprise you. Sorry about scaring you. I wasn't thinking."

"That's for sure." Rachel's gaze darted between the two men. "You still haven't explained why you're here."

"I…I've got bad news." Art looked down at his feet.

"What?"

He raised his head. "You didn't get the part."

Rachel's heart sank. "You came all the way out here to tell me? You could've phoned."

Art grimaced. "I know, but I wanted to make sure you'd be okay. I know how much you wanted it. You've had a lot of bad news lately, and I was worried about your state of mind—"

"You're overly concerned. I'm fine. This isn't the end of the world." Rachel tried to put on a brave face, but her chest ached as if a large hand were squeezing her heart. No matter how much the rejection hurt, she wouldn't cry. She'd cried enough over her mother and all of the other losses in her life. She wouldn't cry over some movie role.

"So when can I expect you back in L.A.?"

"I'm staying here for a while. Since I didn't get the part, there's not much reason to hurry back."

"I hope you're not getting too comfortable here. When you're not making money neither am I."

"You can't fool me with that hard-luck story. You're making plenty of money. You don't need me."

"Yes, I do."

She took in Art's boyish good looks. His dark hair was combed back from his cherubic face. His gray eyes, the color of smoked glass, gazed at her with admiration. "You haven't changed, I see. Still the money man."

"It's about more than money. I really wanted to make sure you're doing okay."

"I said I…I'm doing fine. Becky and I are enjoying the vacation."

"I certainly don't see what you find so appealing about being out here in the boonies."

"Family and friends," she said, admitting to herself how much she'd come to rely on them.

"The country life must agree with you. You're looking good, but I don't know how you can tolerate some of these country smells."

She laughed. "You get used to them after a while. When did you arrive?"

"I actually had a nice visit with your neighbors."

"John and Sarah?"

"Yeah, they were telling me about the area. Seems your friend has the acting bug."

Rachel knit her eyebrows. "What are you talking about?"

"She was telling me about the community theater she works with every year. Sounds quite interesting."

Rachel turned to Matt. "How come Sarah never mentioned her work with the theater?"

"Got me." Matt shrugged. "Maybe she thought it was small potatoes compared to what you do."

Art placed a hand on Rachel's shoulder. "Since you plan on staying for a while, maybe you ought to get involved."

"I don't want to interfere. Besides, it might bring out the reporters."

"The publicity can't hurt."

"I've kind of enjoyed being anonymous."

"That won't last," Art said with a chuckle.

"Well, for now I like things the way they are."

"Come on. You could use some good press after the not-so-flattering stuff about you that's been splashed in the tabloids. That breakup with the latest boyfriend didn't paint a very pretty picture."

"I thought you said there's no bad publicity."

"Yeah, if you're working, any publicity's good. But you aren't working. You know I didn't want you to take time off from your show." Art waved his hand in the air. "Out of sight. Out of mind."

"We've had this discussion. I don't want to talk about it again. I made the decision to take time off, and that's that."

"What if they decide not to bring you back? Your character can be written out of the story faster than you can blink."

Narrowing her gaze, Rachel shrugged. She wouldn't let Art have the satisfaction of knowing his comment bothered her. "Then I'll have all the time off I want."

"Are you saying you aren't ready to work anyway?"

"No, I'll be ready to work when the right thing comes along."

"The right thing is this little theater group." Art stepped closer and put an arm around her shoulders. "You'll be helping out your friend. You'll be helping out the community. Think of it as your good deed with lots of good publicity."

Rachel sighed. Was this the right thing to do? So far in her career, Art had never steered her wrong. What could it hurt? "Okay, you've convinced me. Maybe they'll let me direct."

"Good idea. It will give you another perspective." Art gave her a hug. "I can see the headlines now. 'Community theater gets big boost from TV star Rachel Carr.'"

Leaning against the doorframe between the kitchen and the den, Matt watched the exchange between Rachel and Art. Maybe those tabloid stories were true. She was definitely feuding with her agent right here in front of him. But he'd talked her into doing work for the community theater. Was she using them for her own purposes? He didn't want to believe she was the kind of person who would take advantage. And what about the breakup with latest boyfriend? Matt thought he knew her, but now he wasn't sure. Rachel and Art were definitely two of a kind. Hollywood people. She was so wrapped up in conversation with her agent that he felt like walking out of the house and out of her life. She didn't need him.

"Rachel," Matt called as he stepped toward her. Art and Rachel turned at the sound of his voice. "I'm going to head home."

He could tell by the look in her eyes that she was embarrassed. "You don't need to go." Her voice was barely above a whisper. "Please stay."

Smiling halfheartedly, Matt shook his head. "You've got company and lots of things to talk about." He glanced at Art. "Nice meeting you," he added with a nod before turning to Rachel. "Good night. I can see myself out."

"No, I'll walk out with you." She followed close behind him. "Matt."

He stopped to open the door. "I'm sorry you didn't get the part."

"Me, too, but I'll live," she said quietly. "You really don't have to go. I'm sorry about Art and how crazy I got. It's just that ever since that break-in—"

Matt put his finger to her lips. "It's okay. I understand."

Shaking her head, she closed her eyes and took a deep breath. He couldn't resist gathering her close and holding her. She went willingly into his arms and put her arms around his waist. They stood in silence for several moments. Matt didn't want to say anything for fear of breaking the connection between them.

Even though he wasn't feeling that confident about his standing with Rachel right now, he wasn't going to give up without a fight. "I like being here for you. Remember that. Whenever you need someone, I'll be here. Good times or bad."

She nodded her head against his shoulder. He didn't want to think about the projects Rachel and her agent might discuss— projects that would take her back to L.A. He had planned on asking her for a real date. Did he dare? It was time to quit being a coward. He held her at arms' length. "I'd like to take you to a movie a week from Saturday night in Sioux Falls. Your choice."

"Sure. That sounds like fun, but I'll warn you now. I have to have lots of popcorn when I go to the movies."

"Great. I think I can spring for both the popcorn and the movie." He opened the door. "I'll see you later."

As he walked out the door, he had a little spring in his step, despite his limp. She'd said yes, even though her agent waited inside with an agenda to get her back to California. Could he possibly compete? He should borrow a page from Rachel's book. Take it one day at a time.

Chapter Ten

Even though Matt had asked her to go to a movie, a sense of loss overcame Rachel as he walked out into the moonlit night without a backward glance. She stood in the doorway until his pickup disappeared from sight.

Turning, she bumped into Art. "Sorry."

"Hey, I'm the one who's sorry. I didn't know I was going to be breaking up a romantic evening." He eyed her speculatively. "And then again, maybe I'm not so sorry." His brows rose in a question. "How involved are you with this Matt fellow?"

Rachel released an exasperated sigh as she walked back into the den. Now she had to deal with Art and all of his questions—questions she couldn't answer herself.

"I don't know as that's any of your business."

"I make it my business when it might hurt your career."

"When it hurts my career, then you can ask. I have lots of decisions to make. I'm taking things one day at a time. And you're not going to change my mind." She put up her hand to quiet him. "Let me get you something to drink."

After she served him, they sat in silence for a few moments. Finally, she asked, "Why so quiet?"

"Just thinking. You aren't going to let this guy keep you from coming back to California, are you?"

"I thought we'd already decided to leave my private life private." She frowned at him.

"Okay. You win, but don't let him turn your head. You're too talented to give up your career."

"Are you still living in the dark ages? Women don't have to give up their careers because they fall in love."

"Aha. So you admit you're in love."

"I don't admit anything. If you don't behave yourself and drop the subject, I'll tie you up in the barn."

Art nodded his head. "As an act of self-preservation, consider the subject dropped."

"Good."

"Is it okay to talk about the community theater?"

"I suppose."

"You will get involved, right?"

Rachel nodded. "I'll talk to Sarah, but I'm not making any promises beyond that."

Rachel gathered her CDs and headed for Sarah's house for their scheduled workout session. Art's suggestion about getting involved in the community theater buzzed through her mind. Would Sarah welcome her interest? Sarah's friendship meant a lot, and Rachel didn't want to do anything to jeopardize it.

As Rachel walked on the shoulder of the road, heat rose from the blacktop, signaling a warmer than normal day for early June. Tiny cornstalks in the nearby field rustled in the warm breeze. The sights and sounds reminded her how peaceful her life seemed here on the farm far away from her life in California. Now she wouldn't have to go back for the foreseeable future.

But was she being fair to Matt by going out with him when

she didn't see a real future for their relationship? Going to a movie together sounded so simple, but after a few days of soul-searching that idea seemed destined for heartache. His and hers.

In the distance she heard an approaching vehicle. As it drew closer she turned to look. When she recognized Matt's pickup, her heart did a little flip-flop. All thoughts of heartache scattered. While she was here, it was impossible to resist him.

He stopped beside her and stuck his head out the open window. "Going my way?"

"Are you trying to pick me up?"

"Yeah. You're the best looking woman I've seen all morning."

"Probably the only woman you've seen all morning."

Wrinkling his brow, he pretended to think. "As a matter of fact, you're right."

"You certainly know how to hand out the compliments." She smiled and realized how much this simple teasing lit up her day. She hadn't been this happy in a long time. But how long could it last?

"I work on it really hard." Grinning, he pushed his cap back on his head. "You'd better not stand in the road too long or someone will run you over."

Rachel laughed as she walked around the pickup and got in. "Don't let Sarah know I'm taking a ride. I told her she has to walk over to my house for the exercise. She won't think it's fair."

"I promise I won't tell on you," Matt replied. "Where's Becky?"

"She's spending the day with my Aunt Lois. Why are you out so early?"

"John and I've been working on the tractor since sunup, and

I had to go to town for a part. That one tractor keeps giving out on us." Matt put the pickup in gear and started down the road.

Rachel looked over at him as the morning sun glinted off the windshield. "Are you happy now that Sarah has told you what we've been doing?"

Matt laughed. "Yeah, but I don't know what the big secret was all about."

"I didn't think you'd understand."

"Yes, I do." He slowed the pickup as they entered the drive. "She didn't want to tell us she was trying to lose weight again."

"Your attitude is one of the reasons she didn't want to say anything."

"My attitude? What did I do?"

"You're skeptical. I can tell by the way you said *again*."

"No, I'm not. I'm glad you're trying to help. That's one of the things I like best about you. You're a caring person." Matt brought the pickup to a stop in front of Sarah's house.

Rachel reached over and touched Matt's arm. "I appreciate your compliment, but don't make me out to be a good person."

Matt frowned. "Why not?"

"Because I don't want to have to live up to someone's expectations," Rachel said, knowing how much she wanted Matt's approval but how much she feared falling short. And she would.

Sighing, Matt gazed at her. "None of us is truly good. We all need God's help."

"That's another one of those expectations I can't live up to. I'm no good at all."

"You're being too hard on yourself. God loves you, and I can see His love in you even though you deny it."

Not wanting to look at him, she closed her eyes for a moment. Why couldn't she look at life as he did? She shouldn't let a simple compliment make her feel on edge. Finally turning her gaze on him, she said, "Let's not talk about it."

"Okay, if that's the way you want it."

Rachel got out of the pickup and closed the door. "Thanks for the ride."

"Sure," he said, then drove off toward the barn.

She walked slowly to the house and wondered why he was so perfect. Didn't he ever struggle with anything in life? He seemed to know all the answers.

"Hey, Rachel."

She glanced up to see Sarah standing at the back door. "Did I hear a pickup?"

Rachel smiled despite the sinking feeling in her heart. "You caught me."

"That's all right. I can understand your wanting to be with Matt. I detect a little romance."

"I'm not sure."

"What do you mean?" Sarah opened the door and went inside.

Following her, Rachel wondered whether she could voice her fears and misgivings to Sarah. Would she understand? In Sarah, Rachel saw someone who battled problems in her life, but with Matt there never appeared to be a struggle. She didn't want to compete with that perfection. "I don't know."

"Well, if you don't know. Who does?" Sarah picked up her sweatband and put it on her head. "I thought you two had a romantic time at the wedding and you're going to the movies a week from Saturday. Erin's still planning to have Becky spend the night."

"We did and we are and she is, but I'm not so sure I should go now."

"Why not?"

"Because this romance can't go anywhere."

Sarah pulled out a chair at the kitchen table and pointed at it. "Have a seat. Sounds like you need a little pep talk."

Rachel plopped onto the chair and crossed her arms in front of her. "Are you going to lecture me?"

"No." Sarah gave her a stern look. "This is just friend chatting with friend."

"In other words, a lecture in disguise."

Shaking her head, Sarah laughed. "If you want to look at it that way."

"Okay. As a friend, what are you going to tell me?"

Sarah put her elbows on the table and clasped her hands in front of her. "I don't understand why you and Matt keep fighting the attraction you have for each other. I see the way you're always looking at each other. Talk about spontaneous combustion. I'm just waiting for the flames to start when you're together."

"Yeah, and the flames could die out just like that." Rachel snapped her fingers.

"Is that what you're afraid of? That it won't last?"

"It's too complicated."

"You're afraid of losing your heart?"

Rachel nodded. "Or getting it broken."

"Well, so is Matt."

"How do you know?"

"Has he ever told you about what happened with Amy?"

"No. We've never talked about his past, especially what happened when he went to war. I've always wondered about their broken engagement, but I've been afraid to ask."

"I can't tell you about his time at war, other than his injuries. He definitely avoids talking about that, but I can tell you about Amy." Seemingly reluctant to start, Sarah played with the napkin holder sitting in the center of the table.

"What about Amy?"

"When she came to teach at the high school, she immediately pursued Matt. She made no secret of her interest. Came

to church. Showed up any time Matt was going to be around."
Sarah paused and released a heavy sigh. "Matt seemed oblivi-
ous to her in the beginning, but eventually they began to date.
By Christmas, they were engaged."

"But that still doesn't tell me why they broke their engagement."

"Yeah, I know." Sarah slowly shook her head. "When Matt's
National Guard unit was called up to go to Afghanistan, Amy
wanted to get married before he left. But thankfully Matt said
they should wait until he came back home."

"Did she break the engagement then?"

"No, no. She was the loving fiancée, writing to him almost
every day."

"Then what happened?"

"When he returned injured, scarred, and suffering from
post-traumatic stress disorder, she bailed."

"As soon as he came back?"

"No, not immediately. It was the middle of the summer
when a roadside bomb hit him. He was shipped back to the
U.S., first to Walter Reed, then to a VA hospital in Atlanta, so
he could be close to his parents. Amy went down to Georgia
to be with him." Sarah sighed again. "I'm not sure exactly
what happened, but right before school started, she resigned her
position at the high school. When she came back to get her
things, she told me that the war had changed Matt and he
wasn't the person she'd fallen in love with."

"So she wasn't able to stick with him through his rehab?"
The thought sickened Rachel. She hurt for Matt. Love could
be so cruel when it didn't work out. She'd learned that lesson.
No wonder Matt's mother had warned her away. Did she dare
tell Sarah about that conversation? Even thinking about it
pained Rachel—maybe because she feared everything Matt's
mother said was true.

Sarah shook her head. "It wasn't just that. She also told me she hated living in a small town."

"If she hated living in a small town, why would she want to marry Matt? He loves it here."

"I think she thought she could convince him to leave."

"Then she didn't know Matt very well." As she made the statement, Rachel recognized that his love of this place went right to the heart of why any relationship she hoped to have with him wouldn't work for the very same reason.

How well did she know him? He loved the Lord. He loved the land. He loved to teach. And those things made him the same man that she'd looked up to as a teenage girl with a bad case of puppy love.

"I never thought Amy was right for him from the beginning."

"Then what makes you think I'm right for him? I'm not much for small towns, either."

"But you still care for Matt despite his physical scars. I believe that's something Amy could never live with. That's the real reason she broke the engagement. She hurt him a lot."

Rachel longed to take away Matt's pain, but she didn't see how a relationship with her would do that. She would probably cause him only more grief. She didn't plan to stay. "When I first saw him I was shocked, but now I hardly notice the scars. He's just Matt—the great guy I've always known."

"See what I mean. You care about him. He needs someone like you."

Rachel shook her head. "It would never work. Too many things have changed. Too much time has passed since those days when I used to wish he'd notice me."

"You had a crush on him when you were a kid?"

Rachel smiled halfheartedly. "Yeah. Remember when I told you I thought he was perfect?"

"Yeah, I do, but I didn't connect that with a crush."

"It was a crush all right. Every summer I could hardly wait till he came to visit."

"How'd you feel when he started teaching here?"

"Like I'd never grow up fast enough."

"Did he know you had this big crush on him?"

"Not then. That would've been very awkward for him being a teacher and all."

"You're right, but what about now?" Sarah asked.

"Now is a big question mark."

"Well, from what I've seen when you two are together, I'd say something's going on."

Shaking her head, Rachel laughed. "You don't give up, do you?"

Sarah reached over and patted Rachel's arm. "I'd like to see two people I care about be happy. Matt hasn't done any dating since he came back. I think he's too self-conscious about his injuries. But don't you dare tell him I told you that."

"Your secret's safe with me." Rachel got up and gave Sarah a hug. "What would I do without you to keep me sane?"

"I'll just have to start charging fees for these little sessions."

"Before we got sidetracked on my love life, I was going to ask you about the community theater. How come you never mentioned it to me but told Art about it?"

Sarah shrugged. "I didn't think you'd be interested. It's only local people putting on a few plays each year."

"I'd love to be a part of it."

Sarah's eyes opened wide. "You would? Wow! That's terrific! We have our next meeting this coming Monday."

"Great. I'll be there. Okay, no more wasting time. Let's get to those exercises." Rachel grabbed her CDs and headed for the front porch, hoping that talk of the community theater would somehow push aside thoughts of Matt. A kiss on a beach didn't make a long-lasting love. Tempting as it was to think about a relationship with him, she had to be honest with herself. Matt's mother was probably right, but deep in her heart Rachel didn't want to believe that.

"Do you always cry at the movies?" Matt asked with an indulgent smile as he and Rachel walked out of the movie theater.

"Only at the good ones."

"So on the Rachel Carr rating system, this was a four tissue movie."

Laughing, Rachel playfully punched Matt in the arm as they walked in the warm night air. "Quit making fun of me."

"I'm not making fun. I'm glad you enjoyed it."

"I liked the company more than the movie."

"Me, too," Matt said, opening the door to his pickup.

Soon they were homeward bound on Interstate 90. While the pickup sped by darkened fields and the lights from distant farms, Matt thought about the chance he was taking with Rachel. He couldn't throw this opportunity away, but was he ignoring all of the alarms his mind kept flashing?

"Sarah tells me you've been helping her with the theater," Matt said, breaking the silence and putting his thoughts on a different track.

Rachel nodded. "Yeah. It's a lot of fun, and Sarah's terrific."

"Sarah's kind of a ham. Don't tell her she's good. It might go to her head, and she'll want to take up acting for real."

"It's too late. She's already planning her theatrical debut," Rachel said with a chuckle.

"What do you mean?"

"I told Sarah she should have a part in the new production instead of just working behind the scenes. You should get involved in the theater, too."

"Me? I'm no actor." He turned into her driveway.

"There are plenty of jobs besides acting."

The yard light atop the tall pole cast long shadows as they got out of the car and walked hand in hand toward the house. Crickets sent their overture into the night.

When they reached the door leading into the garage, Matt paused. "Is the door locked tonight?"

"You don't think I'd ignore your advice, do you? You'll notice the new deadbolts." She handed him the key.

He turned the key in the lock. "I was just making sure. I didn't want to be surprised by unexpected visitors again."

"You don't have to worry." Grabbing his hand, she pulled him inside, closed the door behind her and with a quick twist locked the door. "There, that should keep all the bad guys on the outside."

She leaned against the door with her face upturned to him. In the dim light cast from the lamp burning in the den, her eyes searched his face.

"We don't want any intruders," he whispered, his lips close to hers.

"No, we don't." With his hand braced against the door, he leaned forward and gently kissed her.

Abruptly pulling away, she lowered her gaze and rubbed the back of her neck. "Matt…"

"Is something wrong?"

She shook her head. "I don't know. It's you, the farm, God, everything." She gave him a helpless look. "It's coming at me like a tornado, and I don't know what to do."

"I've been called a lot of things but never a tornado." He smiled even though he felt like chewing up a few things in his path. She was saying all of the things that he'd told himself would stand in their way. Why did he want to ignore the warning signs? They all indicated disaster, but he planned to ignore every one of them. He wanted a place in her life. "I'm not a very forceful tornado because I didn't manage to sweep you off your feet."

Rachel smiled at his joke. "You did long ago, when I was a girl."

"Then why are you still standing?" he asked, knowing this lighthearted banter wasn't getting them anywhere.

She took his hand. "Let's go into the den."

Matt followed and joined her on the couch. "What's the problem, Rachel?"

"I thought I had everything figured out. I was taking everything one day at a time. But I realized what I do today affects what happens tomorrow. I can't ignore the future."

"I care about you, and I'm not going away."

Her beauty captured his soul, not only the outer beauty that was so obvious, but the inner beauty as well. He couldn't help thinking how right it would be to have her here every day for the rest of his life. But even if she fell in love with him, she'd be gone half the time with her work. He wasn't sure he wanted that kind of wife. He needed someone to share his life as well as his love of the Lord. So where did that leave them? He didn't have an answer.

"And I don't want you to go away." She touched his arm. "I'm sorry. I just need space to figure this all out."

His heart aching, he looked at her. Space. Yeah, he could give her space, but he still didn't want to give up. "Okay. Maybe it's better this way. We both need space. But is that invitation still open to help with the theater?"

"Sure. If you don't want to act, we can always use stage hands and help making the sets."

"Great," Matt said, willing to accept whatever role Rachel was offering him in her life, for the moment. He wanted to find out if there was a chance for them, but he was afraid to find out it wouldn't work. He tried to convince himself that working together wasn't going to hurt anything.

He would ask for God's guidance to do the right thing, but he was afraid the answer wasn't what he wanted to hear.

Chapter Eleven

While Matt put the finishing touches on a scenery backdrop, he glanced over to where Rachel was helping the actors with their lines. Her involvement in the community theater had sparked a surge of new interest. Even people from nearby towns came for auditions. The group had been practicing throughout the summer in preparation for their opening the third weekend of September, which was only a month away. Under Rachel's direction the musical comedy was coming together.

Matt's original skepticism about her reasons for working with the theater had slowly slipped away. Her disappointment over not getting that movie part seemed forgotten as she threw herself wholeheartedly into helping with the community theater. She'd taken a group of unseasoned performers and guided them until their talents shone. She brought out the best in them. If she hadn't gone into acting, she would've made a great teacher.

He'd learned over the years that students only gave as much as the teacher expected. So he'd always let his students know he expected a lot. Rachel had done the same with these amateur actors, and they reached for their best performances. Week by week a spectacular transformation had occurred right before his eyes.

"Hey, Matt." Rachel's voice shook him from his thoughts. "We need your help."

Matt laid his paintbrush on a nearby paint can and stood. "What do you need?"

Rachel motioned for him to come over to her. "Steve has to leave early, and I want you to read his part."

"Me?" Matt pointed to himself. "I'm no actor."

"I'm not asking you to act, just read." She held out a script to him.

"Isn't there someone else?"

"No. You're it." She shoved the script at him.

Taking it, he stared at the pages. "Who am I supposed to be? I don't have to sing, do I?"

"No singing. You're going to be Leo." Rachel turned back to the other actors.

"Great. That's good for everyone involved, because I can't sing." He chuckled, glanced at the script and hoped he wouldn't make a fool of himself. He didn't want to look stupid in front of all these people, especially Rachel.

Gripping the pages, he waited for his turn. His hands grew clammy. Why was he so nervous? All he had to do was read, but he didn't like being in the spotlight. Being the center of attention in his classroom was about as much attention as he could take.

Then he caught a glimpse of Becky sitting in the nearly empty auditorium. She looked up from the game she was playing and smiled at him. She gave him a little wave. At least he impressed Becky. He was a hero in her eyes. He wished he were a hero in her mother's eyes. He didn't know where he stood with Rachel, so why did he keep torturing himself with trying to impress her?

"Leo. Leo, you missed your cue."

"Sorry." Matt jumped into his part and chided himself for letting his mind wander.

Matt managed to get through the rest of the play without another missed cue. When they did one more run-through, he even put a little inflection into his voice as he read the lines.

"You did good, Matt." Becky hurried toward him. "Mom should put you in the play."

"Thanks, Becky, but I think we'll leave the acting to your mom and those other people. I'm better with paintbrushes, and I've got to clean those before we head home."

"After you do that, can we go for ice cream?" Becky asked.

"Oh, so now we know why she said I did such a good job. She's bribing me to take her for ice cream." Matt winked at Rachel. "What do you think?"

"I think she's right about you doing a good job, and I think the two of you are going to make me fat with all these stops for ice cream."

"Mom, you're not fat."

"I agree."

Rachel laughed. "Thanks for the vote of confidence."

"I meant it. How could you get fat when you do all that jumping around with Sarah?"

"Okay, we can go for ice cream."

"Yippee!" Becky cried, skipping toward the door at the back of the auditorium.

Sitting at a table in front of the Dairy Mart, Matt thought of all the events of the summer that had ended with a trip here for ice cream—the fireworks on the Fourth of July, the Corn Palace Stampede Rodeo in Mitchell, where Becky learned about barrel racing firsthand. He'd offered to take Becky to those events so he could be with Rachel. He was either a coward or not being honest with himself.

There were also church activities. When he learned about Rachel and Sarah's bargain, he made sure he picked Rachel and Becky up for church every Sunday. Although she sat in the pew beside him, he wondered what went through her mind while she listened to the sermon. Did the message of God's love touch her, or did she tune it out? He wished he knew.

Becky shouted with delight as she played with some smaller children, the parents sitting nearby enjoying their ice cream. Several teenagers milled around under the neon sign that flashed a rainbow of colors. Life seemed so simple here. Was it too simple for someone like Rachel? Why couldn't he be satisfied with how their relationship was progressing? The closer they became, the more he was afraid she would decide to go back to California.

"How's the banana split?" Matt asked, trying to get rid of his troubled thoughts.

"Good. There's nothing else like one." Rachel took another spoonful.

"You've certainly been quiet tonight," Matt said, wondering what was on her mind.

"I'm all wrapped up in thinking about the theater. The opening is only a few weeks away. I hope we're going to be ready."

"Everyone's doing great." He chuckled. "As long as you don't have to have me for a stand-in."

"Thanks for helping out tonight."

"Thanks for putting up with me." Matt chuckled. "Have you heard from that agent of yours recently?"

"He won't make any more surprise visits, if you're worried about that."

"I wasn't worried about him, but he seemed pretty eager to get you back to California." Why had he mentioned the guy? He wasn't even here, yet he was intruding on their time together. Matt put his arm around her shoulders. "I don't want you to leave."

"I'm not going anywhere for now." She put her hand on his arm. "Becky will start school here in a week."

His hopes soared. "So you're not planning to leave any time soon?"

"No. I love working with the theater, and I'm not ready to go back, especially now that the movie part didn't materialize."

"But what happens when one does?"

"I can't foretell the future. Let's just think about here and now."

Could he ignore the future? He was torn in too many directions. He was afraid she would leave before he had a chance to see her come back to God. He had such hopes because she was attending church on a regular basis. But he had to face reality. She was going because of her bargain with Sarah. Rachel had made that very clear when he'd asked her about it.

Then there was the selfish part he tried to not dwell on. He wanted to win her heart for himself. He wanted so much to be a part of her life, but if she never came back to the Lord, was he only playing with fire? He had to be honest with himself and true to the Lord. These same things had bothered him since she'd walked back into his life last May.

Rachel slapped her arm. "The mosquitoes are getting wicked out here."

"You're right." Standing, Matt stretched his hands above his head. "Let's go home."

"Okay." Rachel got up from the table. "Becky, we're going."

"Do we have to?"

"Yes, I don't want you to get eaten by mosquitoes."

Giggling, Becky ran toward her mother. "They can't eat me. I'm too big."

"I know, but they can sure make you itch." Rachel waved a hand to shoo away the offending insects.

"If you do what your mother says, maybe we can convince her to go to the state fair in Huron over the Labor Day weekend."

Becky looked at her mom. "Please, Mom, let's go to the fair."

"Okay, but like Matt says, you have to be good."

"I will."

Matt watched Becky skip ahead and knew he was doing it again—using Becky to spend time with Rachel. He wasn't proud of himself, but he did care about Becky. But without her, would Rachel be willing to spend time with him? Whenever the three of them were together, they seemed like family. Did Rachel ever feel that way, too? His mind filled with a mountain of questions.

On the ride home, Matt took in the beauty of the prairie sunset. The fencerows, lone farmhouses and shelterbelts stood as blackened silhouettes against a sky awash in oranges and reds. Did Rachel acknowledge the splendor of God's creation?

When Matt slowed the pickup and turned into the driveway, she looked over at him with a smile. His heart twisted. He loved that smile. He loved everything about her, but the same old question plagued him. Despite his prayers and constant wishes that somehow things would work out between them, nothing had changed in the weeks since their one and only date. How could he pursue this relationship when she didn't share his faith?

The smell of hot dogs, popcorn, and candied apples filled the air as Rachel strolled along the midway at the state fair. Squeals and laughter mingled with the drone of motors operating the rides. She wondered whether she'd ever get to be alone with Matt. He'd left with John as soon as they arrived.

Becky tugged on Rachel's arm. "Come on, Mom. You're walking too slow. Erin and I want to ride on the merry-go-round."

"You'll get to ride." Rachel gave Becky a nudge. "Go stand in line with Erin."

Standing with Sarah, Rachel watched as the little girls found horses and scrambled on them. Loud, bouncy music played as the old carousel lurched forward. Becky and Erin shouted and waved each time they passed.

"The girls are certainly having fun," Sarah said.

Rachel laughed. "I always loved the state fair, but not for the rides. My weak stomach couldn't take that twisting and turning. The merry-go-round was about as much as I could handle."

"You can say that again," Matt said, coming to stand behind her. "When you were in high school, you went on the scrambler. You were green when you got off."

The sound of his voice sent her stomach on a roller-coaster ride to match any at the fair. "I'll have you know I've outgrown my motion sickness."

Matt grinned. "We'll see about that."

"Did you guys get your fill of the latest in farm equipment?" Sarah asked.

"We saw it all." John took off his cap and smoothed his hair before replacing the cap. "If we only had the money to buy it, we could sit back and let the farm run itself."

Before anyone could say another word, Becky and Erin came bounding off the merry-go-round.

"What can we go on next?" Becky asked.

"How about the bumper cars?" Sarah suggested.

"Yeah," the little girls chorused.

While the group made their way toward the bumper cars, Matt caught hold of Rachel's arm and pulled her back to walk with him. "How about after this, just the two of us go on a few rides? We can test your claim that you've outgrown your problem with carnival rides."

Rachel stopped and looked at Matt as the others went ahead. "What ride are you taking me on?"

"My choice."

"Should I trust you?"

"I don't know. Can I be trusted?"

"I'll take a chance." This chance had everything to do with her heart and nothing to do with carnival rides.

"Good. We'll start with the roller coaster."

"Start? I thought you said 'a ride.'"

"That's what you said. Nobody can go on just one. That's not a true test."

"For me it is."

"Not when you're with me." He laughed. "Shall we team up for the bumper cars?"

"Sure." The thought of teaming with Matt for something more serious than bumper cars ran through Rachel's mind.

Matt and Rachel laughed their way through the crashes and jolts on the bumper cars. When they finished, Sarah agreed to watch Becky so Matt could take Rachel on the roller coaster.

"You look like you've survived pretty well, but I was beginning to think my arm would drop off and my hearing would be impaired," Matt said, rubbing his upper arm as the roller coaster came to a stop.

"I think you're exaggerating."

"I don't exaggerate. See the finger marks here on my arm?" He pushed up his sleeve and flexed a bicep.

"No. You just wanted me to look at your muscles."

"They are magnificent, aren't they?" he asked with a Cheshire cat grin.

Rachel took a fake swing at Matt. He ducked to avoid the punch. "Didn't they teach you to swing any better than that in the movies?"

"Yeah, but I didn't want to hurt you." Rachel laughed as she ran ahead.

Trying not to let his limp show, Matt caught up with her. "You still have to ride the Ferris wheel."

"Is this the last test?" she asked.

"If you pass."

"I will."

After the attendant locked them into one of the seats, they slowly ascended as people got on below them.

"I love the view from up here," Rachel said as they neared the top.

"As I recall, you didn't like the seat to move." Giving her a sideways glance, Matt began to rock back and forth.

Rachel tucked her arm in his. "You can't scare me."

"I wasn't trying to scare you, just test you."

"Have I passed?"

"Let's rock the seat a little more." The innocent smile did nothing to hide the mischief in his eyes.

As the motion increased, Rachel released her hold on Matt's arm. Willing herself to be calm, she gripped the bar in front of them. "Do I pass the test when you make this thing turn all the way around?"

"That would be exciting."

"Maybe for you. You can rock all you want in your childish game." Rachel looked straight ahead while they slowly descended on the front side of the Ferris wheel.

Matt burst out laughing. "You may be a great actress, Rachel, but you can't hide those white knuckles."

"So does that mean I've failed?"

Putting an arm around her, he pulled her close and whispered, "No, you pass with flying colors. We've gone around once, and you haven't screamed."

She flashed him an irritated look. "No thanks to you."

"I wasn't expecting thanks, just a kiss."

He leaned over and captured her mouth in a kiss. She forgo the midway and the lights below. The two of them were alon at the top of the world.

When the kiss ended, everything was louder and brighter— the music from nearby rides, the screams and shouts, the lights He pulled her closer. Why had she let him kiss her, when the were all wrong for each other?

When she'd confessed her confusion after their date, he' backed away, agreeing they both needed space. Sure they' worked together at the theater and done the fun stuff with Becky, and of course, attended church together, but he'd kep a certain distance. But that distance had done nothing to help resolve her conflicting emotions.

What was she to make of his behavior now? Was he trying to take her on an emotional roller coaster, as well? Her hear hammered as she gazed into his golden eyes. "What's happening with us?"

"I know I said we'd give each other space, but I can't stop caring about you."

Rachel stared into his wonderful golden eyes and sighed. "I only that could solve everything."

"No matter what you do or where you go, I'll be waiting here for you." He took one of her hands in his. "I can't walk away until I've done everything within my power to share God's love with you."

As the Ferris wheel descended, an unsettled feeling lingered in her stomach. She closed her eyes. He wanted to share God's love with her, but what about his love. Did he want to share that? His kiss should answer that question, but she wanted to cover her ears against his words about God.

Was Matt trying to control her? Her every reason cried ou against the idea. He was her childhood friend. He wasn't like

Dean. Finally, she looked at him. "I'm not sure I deserve God's love."

"We all fall short, but God loves us anyway," Matt replied.

They came to a stop at the bottom of the Ferris wheel. The attendant released them from their seat, giving Rachel no chance to respond to Matt's statement. Grabbing her hand, he maneuvered his way through the crowd. "There's a coffee shop nearby. We can get something to eat and talk this over."

She stopped short, feeling the need to resist what seemed like his attempt to order her around. "What about Becky?"

"She's having a good time with Erin."

"What if I don't want to?"

"Then we won't. I'm not going to make you do anything."

In the waning light, Rachel studied his face. Could she believe him? She was being unfair judging him from her bad experiences, but she couldn't shake the thought. Had her life brought her to the point that she didn't trust him or her own judgment?

She shook her head. "I'm sorry I've been short with you. I'm a little confused."

"You and me both." He reached out and took both her hands. "Let me buy you a piece of cherry pie with a big scoop of vanilla ice cream."

"Okay." Glad that he seemed to understand her discomfort, she fell into step beside him. The last thing she wanted was to hurt him.

After they settled in a booth, the waitress took their order immediately.

"That was quick service," Rachel commented.

"It's because you're the most famous person they've had in here all day." He fiddled with the salt and pepper shakers sitting at the edge of the table.

Rachel glanced around the large open room with booths

lining the walls. In the center, stools covered in bright re
plastic surrounded a long counter. The clicking of silverwar
accented the low hum of conversation. "I don't think anyon
has noticed."

"I—er—wouldn't be too sure about that." Matt looke
toward the back of the restaurant. "Don't look now, but ou
waitress appears to be having an animated discussion wit
several coworkers. I think they've recognized you." Mat
chuckled. "Our order is coming. It's so big it takes three peopl
to deliver it."

"Oh, no." Rachel glanced toward the ceiling. "All this tim
I've managed to avoid being recognized. I guess it couldn'
last forever."

"Smile. Your adoring fans are almost here."

Rachel put on a pleasant face as three young women place
glasses, plates, silverware and napkins in front of them. The
they stood there for a moment as if they were going to watc
Matt and Rachel eat.

Finally, one of them blurted, "Are you Rachel Carr, yo
know that TV actress? I mean, if you're not, you sure look lik
her." Then seemingly embarrassed, she dropped her gaze to th
floor.

Rachel chuckled softly. "Yes, I'm Rachel Carr."

"I can't believe it." The young waitress looked at her friend
and then at Rachel. "Can we have your autograph?"

"Sure." Rachel took the pen and paper they handed to he
"What's your name?" Rachel quickly learned each girl's nam
and signed an autograph for her. Then the threesome disap
peared.

"Luckily, this place isn't very full, or you'd probably hav
to sign a few more of those, wouldn't you?"

"Yeah. Sometimes my private life isn't very private, bu
being on the farm has given me some solitude." Rachel smiled

Over and over again she had to admit that all of the good things on the farm surrounded her and gave her a sense of belonging she hadn't known she missed. Matt was one of those things.

"It's good to see you smile when you talk about the farm." Matt took one of her hands and cradled it between his. "You've had a change of heart about the farm. I hope you'll have the same change of heart about God."

Not able to bear Matt's scrutiny, Rachel closed her eyes. Sometimes, she wanted to share his faith, but she couldn't let go of her doubts. How could God fit into her life again after all this time? Feeling the comforting pressure of Matt's calloused hands, she finally opened her eyes. Warmth radiated from his golden gaze. She didn't want that adoring look to change to one of despair. Hollywood could do that. She wanted to spare him the grief.

With a shake of her head, she stared at him. "I'm not sure that'll ever happen."

"Why do you say that?" A puzzled frown knit his brow.

"You don't know what my life's been like."

"No, I can't say I know what it's like to be rich and famous."

"I'm not talking about that. I'm talking about my personal life." Rachel wondered what Matt would say about the life she'd led. What would he think of her marriage? So many of her fears regarding a new relationship stemmed from her bad experiences with Dean. "You've never asked me about Becky's father."

Matt leaned forward. "I figured you'd tell me when the time was right."

"What do you know about Dean?"

Matt shrugged. "Not much, other than he died doing a stunt in a movie before Becky was born."

Her heart pounded. She should tell Matt about the horrible life she'd lived with Dean. Her shame had kept her from telling anyone. Taking a deep breath, she didn't miss his kind expression. He would understand. "Dean and I met on a movie."

"Was he working as a stunt man?"

"Yes, it was a made-for-TV movie based on a romance novel. He did some of the stunt riding. I had a supporting role."

"I remember Sarah liked that movie," he said with a grin. "John and I watched it only because you were in it."

Rachel smiled despite herself. Matt made her feel wonderful even when the story she was about to tell didn't. "Anyway, one night some guys in the crew were giving me a hard time, and Dean defended me. After that, he was always bringing me flowers or little gifts. He swept me off my feet, and when the movie was finished, we hopped on a plane to Las Vegas and got married. But that kind of whirlwind romance made me fail to see the danger signs."

"Danger? What danger?" Concern shone in his eyes.

"I didn't recognize his possessiveness. I thought I'd fallen in love with a kind, generous and handsome man, but it was all an illusion."

"Why do you say that?" Matt asked.

Shaking her head, Rachel remembered the awful fights. "It didn't take long before I began to see a side of Dean I would come to fear. He was extremely jealous for no reason at all and suspicious of everything I did. Eventually the verbal abuse became physical."

"Why didn't you leave?"

"The first time he hit me, he said he was sorry and it wouldn't happen again. And it didn't, not for a long time. But I lived in constant fear that I would do something to make him angry enough to hit me again. Finally, I did."

"You should've left then."

"I didn't have to. Two days later, he was killed in that accident." Placing her elbows on the table, Rachel let her head rest in her hands. "How can God love me when I wasn't sorry my husband died? I pretended I was, but it was all a lie."

Quickly, Matt got up and slid into the booth beside Rachel. He put his arm around her shoulders. "God forgives our sins. We just have to ask."

"I haven't forgiven myself. How can I ask God to forgive me?" Rachel raised her head and gazed at Matt. "You have such confidence in God, but I don't. I don't know if I ever will."

"Don't be afraid to let God forgive you," Matt said still holding her close.

Rachel let out a shaky breath. "I've lived a life too far from God. How can He ever take me back?"

"I reminded you once before of the Prodigal Son? You can always come home to God no matter how far you've strayed."

Sadly, Rachel shook her head. "I don't know what it'll take to bring me back home."

Chapter Twelve

A gentle breeze rustled the tall cornstalks in the nearby field as Rachel sat between Matt and Becky at a table in the church-yard.

Rachel glanced at Becky's plate. "Do you have enough food?"

Becky nodded. "I wish we could have potluck every Sunday."

"Not me. I'd never stay on a diet." Sarah laughed. "I had enough trouble last weekend resisting all the goodies at the fair."

Matt gave Becky a high five. "I'm with you, kid. These potlucks are great."

Taking in the jovial conversation, Rachel remembered how she'd dreaded going to church after her mother's funeral. Now she was beginning to feel a part of this fellowship. With each passing Sunday, her old fears were losing their grip. Matt's belief in her, Sarah's friendship and Becky's little prayers were chipping away at her resistance to God.

Even words from today's sermon stuck in her mind. Something about God being patient and wanting everyone to come to repentance. Sometimes, she wanted to believe, but some unknown fear held her back.

"Mom, when do we get to do the corn maze?" Becky's question startled her from her thoughts.

"After we eat."

"I can hardly wait." Becky clapped her hands.

Rachel looked at Matt. "When did they start this corn maze thing?"

"A few years ago. Since Carl's a church member and his field adjoins the church property, he opens up his maze to us every year."

"So are you good at this?" Rachel asked.

"Sometimes. This small maze is nothing compared to some of the big mazes east of here. Those are spectacular." Matt looked at the sky. "We have perfect weather for it."

"Yeah, we'd better enjoy it while we can. There's supposed to be a big front coming through here later in the week," John said. "Hope we don't get any bad storms."

After the potluck meal, Rachel, Becky and Matt ventured into the maze along with John, Sarah, Erin and other church members. Soon laughter and shouting sounded through the cornstalks. Matt took Rachel's hand, and she smiled. She didn't want to think about anything that would take this feeling of contentment away.

Becky and Erin skipped through the maze in front of the adults. Rachel, Matt, John and Sarah moseyed along the path between the cornstalks.

"Do we know where we're going?" Rachel asked.

Matt grinned. "To the end."

Turning, Rachel gave him an irritated look. "That was a smart-aleck remark."

"Just the truth."

"Don't get him started. He'll just get worse," Sarah said.

When Rachel turned around, she didn't see Becky. Her heart jumped into her throat. "Becky, where are you?"

There was no response.

"She has to be right ahead of us. She and Erin were here just a minute ago." Matt hurried around the next corner.

Rachel followed close behind him. "There's Erin."

The four adults rushed ahead. Erin came back to meet them. "I can't find Becky."

"What happened to her?" Rachel tried to tamp down the panic. Nothing would happen to her. It was only a corn maze.

Erin shook her head. "I'm not sure."

"Becky!" Rachel yelled. There was no answer. She looked at Matt. "Why doesn't she answer? Becky!"

Matt put an arm around her shoulders. "We'll find her."

"Is someone lost?" A shout sounded from another part of the maze.

"Yes. We can't find Becky." Rachel tamped down her fear.

More voices sounded through the maze, as they called Becky's name.

Finally, Rachel heard Becky's little voice. "Mom, I'm over here."

Sighing with relief, Rachel put a hand over her heart. "Stay right there. We'll find you."

Rachel raced around several corners until she found Becky. She gathered Becky in her arms. "How did you get lost?"

"I don't know. I was with Erin, and then I couldn't find you. I couldn't see anyone."

"Becky, you scared me."

"Mom, you shouldn't worry. You should pray. That's what I did. The memory verse we had in Sunday school this morning said, 'Is any one of you in trouble? He should pray.'"

Matt hunkered down next to Becky. "You're right. We should pray, but I think you should hold my hand until we get out of the maze."

Rachel watched Becky skip ahead with Matt, seemingly

unfazed. Rachel wondered whether she needed what Becky had—a childlike trust that God would see her through. What would make her reach out and grab it?

Warm, humid air greeted Rachel as she rushed out of the theater. Eager to get home, she maneuvered her car out of the parking lot. She'd stayed behind to take care of some last minute business. Sarah had gone ahead to pick up Becky and Erin after school.

Dark clouds on the horizon gave a foreboding look to the landscape. Halfway home, the sky opened up and pounding rain made the windshield wipers useless. She pulled the car off to the side of the road, but the rain left zero visibility and made a deafening sound. Then she realized it wasn't just rain. Marble-sized hail pelted her car.

Then, as suddenly as the storm started, it stopped. Rachel surveyed the scene before her. At first glance, the white covering the ground looked like snow, but the icy pellets told a different story. She opened the door and stepped out. Dents and dimples in the roof and hood of her car showed the destructive force of the hail. Easily fixed, she supposed. At least there was no tornado.

After getting back into the car, she continued her journey home. Hailstones covered the fields ahead. The sunlight, trying to break through the clouds, cast an iridescent glow on the mounds of icy marbles.

As she neared the turnoff for the farm, she noticed uprooted trees in an adjacent shelterbelt. A tornado must have touched down close by. Worried, she drove faster. She breathed a sigh of relief when her house and the barn came into view in the distance. As she drew closer, she slowed the car and surveyed the area. Tree limbs and leaves littered the lane and farmyard, but nothing looked damaged.

Hoping for the best, Rachel drove toward the Dalton farm. Along the blacktop road, twisted fences and trees lay everywhere. Gripping the steering wheel tighter, she pressed the accelerator to the floor. Her heart pounded. She tried to compose herself, knowing she'd seen destruction on the road before she came to her own farm. Everything had been fine there.

But when she had to stop and pull a small tree from the road, Rachel's calm assurance began to waver. Anxiety crept into her mind as she viewed the increasing damage.

As she drew closer, she could see the red barn, but her relief was short-lived. Her deepest fears materialized. No houses appeared on the horizon. Her heart went into her throat as she turned into the lane.

"No, no, no, no, no!" she screamed, stopping the car. She jumped out, not bothering to shut off the engine. The houses were nothing more than a pile of rubble. Rachel ran around like a mad woman, slinging aside the debris and sobbing at the same time. "Becky, where are you?"

Tears ran down Rachel's cheeks. Sobbing, she continued her frantic search in the pile of boards, broken furniture, and shingles for any signs of life.

"Becky has to be safe." She covered her mouth with one hand in order to stifle another sob. She couldn't lose her child.

Her legs nearly gave out as she continued to look through the rubble. Her hands shook, but she made them search through the mess. Fear pumped the adrenaline through her body, pushing her on when she felt like giving up. But she remembered Becky's words. "Mom, you shouldn't worry. You should pray."

Putting her hands over her face, she fell to her knees and prayed. "Dear God, I know I don't deserve Your help, but please make Becky safe. My life is Yours if You do."

A faint cry interrupted her prayer. She heard Becky's

voice. Rachel laughed and wept at the same time. "Becky, where are you?"

"Mom, I'm over here."

Rachel stood and whirled around. On wobbly legs, she ran across the littered ground. When she reached her daughter, she picked her up and held her tight. Tears flowed. "You're safe. You're safe."

"We hid underground."

"Where underground?"

"In the root cellar near the barn," Sarah answered, looking around, horror written on her face.

Setting Becky on the ground, Rachel embraced Sarah, then stepped back. "I'm so sorry. When I saw the houses, I was so afraid…" She closed her eyes against the destruction. When she opened her eyes again, she realized only Becky, Sarah, and Erin were there. "Matt, John. Where are they?"

"Matt came home from school and went out to help John with the harvest. They're out in the fields. I…" Sarah broke into tears. "We have to find them. Everything's gone."

Rachel embraced her friend and patted her back as she shared in her sorrow, then turned toward the car. "Let's go."

Nodding, Sarah wiped the tears from her face. "They're supposed to be working in the acreage over on the west side of the main road."

"Get in my car. It's going to be all right," Rachel said, trying to reassure herself as well as Sarah. Her words gave little comfort when her friend had lost almost everything.

When everyone was in the car, Rachel cautiously turned around, avoiding tree limbs, boards, and other debris scattered across the farmyard. Before she reached the end of the drive, two tractors came into view. Rachel stopped the car, and the four females catapulted from the car and dashed toward the men.

Seeing Matt, Rachel raced into his arms. He was soaking wet, but he was alive. Tears flowed again when he put his strong arms around her. "You're safe."

"Hey, don't cry. It's okay," Matt said, wiping the tears from her face with a callused hand.

Sniffling, Rachel smiled through her tears. "I know you're okay, but look at the houses. They're destroyed."

Matt looked at Sarah and John with determination. "We have insurance. We can rebuild. The barn's still standing, and we haven't lost any equipment."

"The important thing is we're alive," John said.

Feeling a tug on her arm, Rachel glanced down to find Becky peering at her with concern. "Mom, is our house okay?"

Rachel nodded. "Everything's fine at our place, honey."

"That's good news," Matt said.

Despite his positive words, Rachel didn't miss the concern etched across his brow. "We ought to salvage whatever we can here before dark. Then everyone can stay at my place."

Her lower lip quivering, Sarah came over to Rachel and hugged her again. "Thanks. I'm sorry I keep crying."

"Don't be sorry. It's the natural thing to do," Rachel said. "Let's get to work."

Hand in hand, Sarah, John and Erin walked toward the pile of debris that had once been their home. Despite Rachel's resolve, tears welled in her eyes as she watched them.

Matt put an arm around Rachel's shoulders. "They'll recover. We'll recover. There's no need to cry."

"Yes, there is." Rachel blinked, and a tear rolled down one cheek. She reached up to wipe it away.

"Let's help John and Sarah." While Becky clung to Rachel, Matt grabbed her hand and led the way toward the shattered remains of John and Sarah's house.

Rachel stopped, bringing them to a halt. "Shouldn't you get out of those wet clothes?"

"What would I put on?" Matt asked, looking around him at the twisted remains of his house.

Rachel bit her lip, then sighed. "I wasn't thinking. Maybe we have something over at my place you can use. I'll check."

When Rachel returned, she found everyone, including Becky and Erin, searching the remains of John and Sarah's house. She brought back some old clothes she'd found in the basement. While she helped Sarah continue the search, Matt and John changed in the barn.

During the next couple of hours, cries of triumph mingled with cries of anguish as they waded through the ruins. They found treasured items unharmed and others destroyed. Luckily, Matt had parked his pickup near the barn. John and Sarah weren't as fortunate. A tree had smashed the roof of their car. Their pickup lay upside down in the yard. Using Matt's pickup, they hauled salvageable furniture and goods to the barn for storage.

While they were searching for clothes they could take to Rachel's to wash, the sheriff came by. After stopping his car, he slowly got out. He walked toward them shaking his head.

"Hey, John, is everyone all right here?"

John nodded as he quit working. "Yeah, but as you can see we've lost the houses. How's the rest of the county look?"

"So far the only damage I've seen other than trees and crops is the Ericksons' barn. Their house was spared. But there may be more damage south of here."

"You guys have a place to stay?"

Matt came forward. "We're staying at Rachel's."

"Good. When news gets out about the damage here, there'll be lots of people over to help. I'll start spreading the word," Steve said as he headed back to his car. "I'll be in touch." Waving, he drove away.

They worked until darkness stole across the prairie and they could no longer see. Dirty, hungry and tired, they trooped into Rachel's house.

Stopping in the kitchen, Rachel surveyed the motley crew. "Let's see. We have to decide where to put everyone. Sarah and John can take the bedroom at the back. Erin can bunk with Becky." Rachel glanced helplessly at Matt. "And Matt will have to take the love seat in the den. It pulls out into a bed."

"Hey, it could be worse. I could be sleeping on the floor," Matt replied with a chuckle.

"I'm hungry, Mom. What can we eat?" Becky asked.

"I've got frozen pizzas. I'll pop them in the oven."

While they ate, neighbors, relatives and people from church called to see what they could do to help. Rachel's Uncle Henry stopped by the house to say he was organizing a work party to help with the cleanup the next day.

When her uncle left, Rachel turned to Matt. "You and John should probably call your parents and let them know what happened."

"I don't know if we should upset them."

"Your folks will want to know you're safe and what happened to the houses. They'll be more upset if you don't tell them."

Matt sighed. "You're right. I'll get John, and we'll make the calls. I should also call the school for a substitute tomorrow and Friday. That way I'll be free to help with the cleanup."

After they made the phone calls and everyone had showered, the girls went to bed and the adults settled in the den to watch the news on TV. The tornado was the top story. While they were viewing the destruction shown on the news, Becky came into the room.

"Mom, I can't sleep," she said, curling up in Rachel's lap.

Rachel brushed the hair from Becky's face. "Is Erin sleeping?"

Becky nodded her head. "I tried to sleep, but I can't."

"Well, you can sit here with me for a while. Try to rest," Rachel said as she cradled Becky in her arms.

Information about the tornado continued on the news. The reports came in from several nearby counties where the twisters had touched down. The picture showed that the worst loss of property and life took place in a small community about thirty miles southwest of them. The twister had almost destroyed the town.

As the pictures rolled across the television screen, Rachel realized Becky was clinging more tightly. "I'm taking Becky back to her bedroom. I'll stay with her until she falls asleep." Rachel got up and put Becky on the floor. "Say good-night to everyone."

Becky went around the room giving everyone a good-night kiss as if she was trying to prolong her stay. Then she reluctantly left with Rachel.

When Rachel returned a half hour later, Matt was sitting alone flipping back and forth between two late-night shows. "Has everyone else gone to bed?"

"Yeah, and left me all alone. Did Becky go to sleep?"

Rachel nodded. "She's really shaken by all this."

"Did she say that?" Matt asked with concern.

"No, but I sensed it. I'm afraid she's taking this too hard. You'd think it would be Erin. Her house is gone."

"It'll probably hit Erin tomorrow." Motioning for Rachel to sit next to him, he clicked the remote control. The TV screen went black. The ticking of the mantel clock echoed in the quiet.

As she settled beside him on the old plaid sofa, the day's events went through her mind. She shuddered. Things could have been so much worse. This was the first chance she'd had to contemplate the situation.

She remembered her prayer. Becky was safe. She had to

admit she'd changed from doubting God to asking Him to save her little girl. Maybe bargaining with God wasn't the right thing to do, but she'd made that bargain. He had kept His end. Now she had to keep hers.

Rachel glanced at Matt. "I made a promise to God today."

Sitting forward, Matt turned to look at her. "You did what?"

"When I saw the destruction from the tornado, I prayed. I promised God that if He kept Becky safe, I'd turn my life back to Him."

Grinning, Matt put his arm around her shoulders. "You don't know how happy this makes me. My prayers are answered, too."

"I'm only sorry it took a tragedy to bring me to my senses."

"Let's just think about the good things tonight." Putting both arms around her, he pulled her close. The emotions of the day spilled over into their embrace.

She pulled away. "Matt…"

"I know," he said huskily, "we'd better stop."

"Hopefully a new day will bring better things." Rachel relaxed against him as she let out a long, slow sigh. Laying her head on his shoulder, she felt safe and secure. Somehow things would work out between them.

The next morning Rachel tiptoed through the den. She looked lovingly at Matt who still slept on the foldout bed that was too small for him. The blanket and sheet lay twisted about him. His foot stuck out from under the covers and hung over the edge. Tempted to tickle it, she resisted the urge and continued toward the kitchen.

The sun shining brightly in the clear blue sky belied the destruction that had taken place yesterday. Her heart ached for Matt, John, Sarah and Erin, who would face their loss again today. She quickly went to work preparing breakfast for her houseguests.

Rachel and Sarah helped Becky and Erin get ready for school. After the girls got on the school bus, the adults drove over to the Dalton farm. Rachel was glad that Becky wouldn't have to see the devastating scene again after the way she'd reacted last night.

Despite all the work they'd done the previous day, the area looked as if no one had touched it. The task before them seemed too great to tackle.

"Where do we start?" Rachel asked.

"Let's do what we were doing last night, trying to find salvageable items." Matt took Rachel's hand and walked toward the mess that had once been John and Sarah's house. "Thanks for coming."

"You don't have to thank me. I'm glad I could be here."

Within an hour, people from town and from neighboring farms began arriving to lend a hand in the cleanup. The air was crisp with a hint of autumn, a sharp contrast from the day before. Folks worked hard, swiftly moving aside debris and saving anything that looked useful for rebuilding. With the help of many hands the task that had seemed insurmountable earlier began to look as if it could be accomplished.

Around noon, Rachel invited everyone over to her place for food prepared by women from their church. People exchanged hugs and condolences with the Daltons as they ate at a hodgepodge of tables set up in Rachel's yard. She realized again that tragedy brought out the best in these people. They'd taken time from their own work to help their neighbors.

When the girls arrived home from school, Rachel met them at the bus stop. "Hi, how was your day?"

"Everyone was talking about the tornado at school," Erin said, skipping beside Rachel. "And I told them how we went into the root cellar till it was over. And how everything was blown everywhere when we came out."

Rachel glanced over at Becky. "What did you tell the class?"

Shrugging, Becky shuffled down the lane. "Nothing. Erin told it all."

Erin stopped skipping and looked at Rachel. "The teacher asked her, but she didn't say anything."

"I didn't want to talk today," Becky mumbled.

Rachel put her arm around Becky and pulled her close. "That's okay. Sometimes it's kind of hard to talk about stuff like that."

"Where's my mom?" Erin asked.

"She's still helping your dad and Matt." Rachel opened the door to the kitchen. "Do you girls want a snack?"

"Yeah." Erin rushed to the kitchen table.

"Wash your hands, and I'll get you some cookies."

Rachel put the cookies on a plate and placed it on the table. Erin quickly grabbed a cookie and started munching on it. "These are good. I love chocolate chip cookies."

"My Aunt Lois made those. You'll have to tell her how good they are when she comes over in a few minutes. She's going to watch you girls while I go back and help."

Leaving her cookie on the table, Becky jumped up and ran to Rachel and threw her arms around her. "Mom, I don't want you to go."

"Honey, you like staying with Aunt Lois."

"But not today." Becky hugged her tighter. "I don't feel so good."

Rachel put her hand to Becky's forehead. "You aren't warm. So you must not have a fever. Why don't you feel good?"

"I don't know," Becky groaned.

"You can lie down for a little bit. Maybe that will make you feel better."

"Stay with me."

"Okay, but when Aunt Lois comes, I have to go." Leading

Becky to the couch in the den, Rachel didn't miss the concern in her daughter's voice.

Becky rested until Aunt Lois arrived. When Rachel tried to leave, Becky clung to her. "Mommy, please don't go."

Rachel hunkered down next to Becky. "Honey, Aunt Lois will take good care of you, and I won't be gone long."

Aunt Lois placed an armload of boxes on the coffee table. "Becky, I brought some of those games with me. You and Erin and I can play them, and your mom will be home before you know it."

Becky appeared somewhat unconvinced but helped Aunt Lois and Erin pick out a game. Lois got Becky involved in setting up a game, then motioned for Rachel to leave. She was torn between helping Matt and staying with her child, but she knew Becky would be in good hands. The storm was over. She couldn't let it continue to bother her.

Rachel, Matt, Sarah, and John worked until sundown as they loaded things into the pickup. After they made the last trip to the barn, Matt made one last perusal of the remains of his house. Looking toward the property, he kicked a broken board nearby.

With most of the debris carried away, the foundation and the plumbing from the first floor bath in Matt's house stood silhouetted against the reddening sky. He removed his cap and ran his fingers through his hair. Cap still in hand, he let his arm fall to his side. His shoulders slumped. He looked weary.

What was he thinking as he surveyed the remains of that house? She wanted to make everything better for him, but she knew she couldn't.

With a heavy heart, she stood beside him. "We got a lot accomplished today," she said, hoping to brighten her own mood as well as his.

He put his arm around her shoulders and drew her close. "It does look manageable now."

"How soon before you start to rebuild?"

"Right away. We need to get started in time to have things under roof before cold weather strikes."

"I gathered from what I heard today that you'll have lots of help."

"Yeah. We've got some decisions to make. Our insurance agent was out today, and he confirmed what I already knew. We won't be able to rebuild both houses."

"Why not? Weren't they both insured?"

"They were, but when John and Sarah made improvements in their house over the years we didn't increase the coverage. It was such a dump before they moved in. It wasn't worth much."

"What will you do?"

"We'll probably rebuild the big house and maybe add a room. It was kind of a waste for me to live in the big house all by myself anyway. We'll make a cousin-in-law suite instead of a mother-in-law suite." Matt laughed halfheartedly.

Rachel forced herself to laugh at Matt's attempt at humor. She wanted to beg him to pick up and move to California with her, but there was no use thinking about it. Asking him to leave was inconceivable.

Chapter Thirteen

Matt tossed and turned on the foldout bed. He wished he could attribute his sleeplessness to the uncomfortable bed, but he knew otherwise. His mind whirled thinking about the destruction. Becky had had nightmares earlier in the evening, but he couldn't sleep at all. When he'd renegotiated the loan for the farm, he hadn't counted on something like this. His optimism sank whenever he considered talking to the bank again. Maybe it wouldn't be necessary.

Finally giving up on the idea of sleep, Matt wandered into the kitchen and opened the refrigerator. Its light dimly illuminated the kitchen. While he perused the refrigerator's contents, he heard footsteps. Looking up, he saw John coming through the door.

"Got the munchies?" John asked.

Matt shook his head. "Couldn't sleep. I keep thinking about the loss of the houses and what it's going to mean."

"Me, too." John joined Matt in front of the refrigerator. He picked up a package of sliced turkey, then looked at Matt. "You know they say turkey has some kind of stuff in it that makes you sleepy. Should we give it a try?"

Matt couldn't help smiling. His cousin always seemed to have a way to lighten the situation. Matt flipped on the light over the sink. "Sure. Let's make a sandwich and have a glass of milk. That's supposed to help, too."

"Yeah, I've heard that." John grabbed a loaf of bread and some mayonnaise. "You want lettuce?"

"Sure. I can't believe we're doing this. I never eat in the middle of the night." Matt got glasses from the cupboard and poured milk while John made the sandwiches.

"There's a first time for everything." John put the sandwiches on plates and brought them to the kitchen table.

Matt joined John at the table. "What's this mess going to do to the farm?"

Running a hand across his rumbled hair, John sighed. "This could be a real setback. And we don't have any of the crop or livestock sale records. The computer, files—gone."

"We can go on without the records, but what about the low insurance money? How will we cover our losses?"

"Some of the church elders talked to me today about taking up a special offering next Sunday."

"But most of the church members here are farmers, and they're struggling, too. We can't expect them to give money they don't have." Matt shook his head, then took a bite of his sandwich.

"They want to do this."

"It's not right to take their money."

"Matt, whether you like it or not, we need help. Why don't you want their help?" John's expression painted a picture of frustration.

"Because we can get by without putting a burden on someone else. I don't want to be indebted to these people."

John shook his finger at Matt. "Someday the tables might be turned, and they would need our help. Don't let pride stand in the way of their generosity and willingness to give. They want to do it. Your I-can-do-all-by-myself attitude helps no one."

Taken aback, Matt looked at his cousin. Easygoing John never made critical statements. Maybe it was the pressure and tension of the past two days. But John had him pegged. Matt had always felt the need to prove to everyone that he could stand up for himself. Maybe it was being the middle brother. Maybe that's why he'd moved so far away from home and done something completely different with his life. He wanted to show people that he was his own man, not just one of those Dalton boys.

Grimacing, Matt shrugged. "I still don't feel good about taking their money."

Smiling, John clapped Matt on the back. "Sometimes you're just hardheaded."

"Not anymore than you," Matt replied, smiling in return.

Taking another bite of his sandwich and a drink of milk, he thought about the work ahead. He hated feeling needy. John was correct. The notion of having to rely on someone else didn't set right with Matt. He wanted to forge his own way. Again he was leaving God out of the picture. The Christian life was all about relying on God, and these people were part of God's plan.

Matt and John finished eating their sandwiches in silence while the refrigerator hummed in the background. The mantel clock in the den chimed the hour. Two o'clock. Matt hoped the turkey and milk would eventually induce the sleep he needed.

When they finished John leaned back in his chair and laced his hands behind his head. "Sarah tells me Rachel made a decision to turn her life back to the Lord. That's great."

"Yeah, it is." Matt smiled, knowing how happy that made him.

"So what's standing in your way now?" John gave Matt a speculative glance.

"What do you mean?"

"I mean with Rachel."

"I don't have anything to offer her. Especially now. And right now we have the farm to think about."

"The farm will always be here. Rachel won't. I've never butted into your business before—"

"Well, this is a bad time to start," Matt interrupted as he stood up and pushed his chair in. He took his plate and glass to the sink. He didn't want to hear any more advice.

John followed. "You're going to let her get away again. She doesn't care about material things. All she wants to hear is that you love her. That'll be enough."

"I'll do things in my own way and in my own time. It's late and thankfully I'm getting sleepy. So let's call it a night."

"Okay. If that's the way you want it. But you're showing how hardheaded you can be," John said as he made his way back to the bedroom.

Matt turned off the kitchen light and fumbled his way back into the den. He lay back on the bed and closed his eyes. His body was weary, but his mind raced with thoughts of Rachel. What he had thought was the main obstacle to their relationship was gone, but now the real obstacle in his own mind reared its ugly head.

Fear.

Fearful that she would never be satisfied being married to a man who wasn't whole, he was afraid to ask for her love because he might fail.

The next morning while getting a reluctant Becky off to school, Rachel recalled Matt and John's conversation about their financial problems. She'd gone to the kitchen for a drink of water, but scurried back to bed after accidentally overhearing a snippet of their heated words.

Matt was obviously too proud to ask for help even when help was offered. She had planned to give them money herself. Now she knew the money had to come from another source. Taking her money would wound Matt's pride. She needed to get advice from Uncle Henry.

She drove over to her uncle's farm, stopping her car near the house as he came up from the barn. When he drew near, she got out of the car.

He walked over and gave her a hug. "It's good to see you. What brings you by?"

"I need to talk to you about something."

He put his hand to her back. "Then let's go inside."

When they came in the kitchen door, Rachel's Aunt Lois turned from the stove where she was baking. "Rachel, what a pleasant surprise! Would you like something to drink? Tea? Coffee?"

"Some hot tea would be great." Rachel sat on one of the old colonial-style chairs situated around a maple table. While she sipped her tea, she told Uncle Henry about her ideas for a fundraiser, and her thoughts on Matt's pride.

Nodding, Henry replied, "We farmers are a proud lot. It's sometimes hard to admit our struggles when we need help."

"I saw that in my dad. He didn't want to let anyone know he was having problems."

"It's better now, but we all need help from time to time. That's why everyone wants to help the Daltons."

"I know, and I thought if we helped more than just the Daltons, it wouldn't hurt their pride. Can we get the names of others who lost property in the tornado?"

"I should be able to do that."

"Thanks, Uncle Henry. On Sunday, I'd like to say something to the congregation at the end of the service," Rachel added.

Her uncle nodded. "I'll make sure you get a chance to speak."

* * *

Sunday dawned bright and clear. Rachel prepared for church with eager anticipation. She marveled at the change in her attitude since that first Sunday after her mother's funeral. That day seemed a lifetime ago. God made everything better.

During the service the music sounded sweeter, the prayers more dedicated and the sermon more interesting. Even with Becky's problems, God filled Rachel's heart with a peace she couldn't deny. She glanced at Matt who sat beside her. He was the only unanswered part of the puzzle.

What did Matt want? He said he cared, but what did that really mean? Was his caring only about her turning her life back to God? She couldn't answer these questions. *God, please help me know what you have in mind for me and Matt.*

At the end of the service, Uncle Henry went to the pulpit for the announcements. He explained to the congregation about the special collection they would take for the families in the area who had lost property in the recent storms.

Finally, he looked at Rachel and motioned for her to come forward. "Before we have our closing prayer, my niece, Rachel, would like to say something."

Rachel walked to the front of the auditorium and took the microphone. "I wanted to let you know how much you've done for me. First, I want to thank you for being here for me when my mother died. You've helped me through a difficult time. Most of all I want to thank you for the prayers you've said on my behalf over the years."

Rachel felt the tears gather in her eyes. She stopped for a moment to collect her composure. Taking a shaky breath, she continued. "When I left ten years ago, I turned my back on God. I wanted to let you know that through your prayers and the gentle persuasion of friends, I've turned my life back to the Lord. Please keep me in your prayers."

When Rachel went back to her seat, Matt took her hand and squeezed it, then held it as Henry asked them to stand for the closing prayer. He prayed for Rachel and all of the families who'd suffered losses. During the prayer the strength of Matt's hand reminded her of how much he'd done for her, but she wanted more. She didn't know how to make that happen.

After the prayer, many from the congregation surrounded Rachel and offered her their congratulations. There were hugs and handshakes and pats on the back. While she accepted their best wishes, she only wished that somehow she could understand Matt's intentions. Maybe his only intention had always been to see her in this situation—back with the Lord.

Sunday evening Sarah, John, Matt and Rachel sat in the den while the guys watched football on TV. Suddenly screams coming from the back of the house made Rachel jump up.

"It sounds like Becky." Rachel ran back to the bedroom with Matt following close behind. They met Becky in the hallway, tears streaming down her cheeks.

"What's the matter, honey?"

"I had a bad dream." Becky clung to her mother.

"What did you dream?" Rachel rubbed Becky's back.

"I don't know, but it scared me."

"It was only a dream. You'll be okay. You need to get some sleep now."

"Stay with me, Mom."

Picking Becky up, Rachel glanced at Matt. "Check on Erin and see if she's still asleep. I'll take Becky to my room."

"Okay."

Rachel went into her bedroom and sat in the rocker in the corner. Only the light from the hallway shone in the room. Rachel pulled Becky into her lap and rubbed her back. "Go to sleep now, honey. Everything's going to be okay."

Becky snuggled close as Rachel rocked back and forth. "Where's Matt?"

"Right here." Matt stood silhouetted in the doorway. "Erin's still sound asleep. That kid can sleep through anything. Sarah went to check on her, too."

"Can Matt read me a story?"

Rachel nodded. "A short one."

Rachel listened to the rise and fall of Matt's voice as he read. She wanted to memorize the sound. She wanted to hear it every day and wake up to it in the morning, but was that dream possible? She didn't dare to hope.

While Matt read, Becky fell asleep in her arms. After he finished, he looked up. "She's sleeping. That's good. You want me to pick her up so you can get out of the chair?"

Rachel nodded. Matt's strong arms lifted Becky from Rachel's lap, and he laid her on the bed. Rachel tucked her in, then stepped back to look at her sleeping child. She appeared so peaceful, but how long would it last?

While Rachel stood there, she considered her daughter's attachment to Matt. She wanted a dad in her life. Could it happen now? The one big barrier that had stood between her and Matt had been torn down like the houses on the Dalton farm. But all the other little things still lay strewn in their path like the rubble left by the storm's destruction. They hadn't had time to talk about it, and with Matt teaching school during the day and working on the house at night, she wondered whether they would get that chance.

While she stood there, Matt came up behind her and put his arms around her shoulder. "She should be okay."

Rachel nodded. That's the way she felt about Matt. She was okay when he was here. Closing her eyes, she sank back into his embrace. Taking in a long, slow breath, she drank in the comfort and strength of his nearness.

* * *

Becky's nightmares continued even though Rachel slept with her every night. Nothing anyone said or did helped. Rachel worried that this was growing beyond something she could deal with. Her worries multiplied when she received a note from Becky's teacher, requesting a conference.

While Sarah watched the girls, Rachel drove to the old brick school building where she'd also gone to school. Inside, the tile floors waxed to a shine and the new coat of paint on the walls did little to hide the building's dumpy, outdated appearance.

At the end of the hall, Rachel found Becky's classroom. Stepping into the room, she saw a young woman seated at the teacher's desk. She looked so young. Rachel suddenly felt older than her years.

The young woman glanced up with a smile, then stood. "Hello, Ms. Charbonneau, I'm Kristin Weiss, Becky's teacher."

"Hello, I'm glad to meet you." Rachel shook the young woman's hand.

"Have a seat right here." Kristin indicated a chair next to hers.

Clutching her purse, Rachel took a seat. "Is Becky having some kind of problem?"

"I was hoping you could tell me what is troubling her." The young teacher looked concerned. "At the beginning of the year, Becky was very eager to learn. She was one of my brightest students. She always volunteered and finished her work ahead of the others. Now she seldom talks in class. She spends much of her time staring out the window. Daydreaming, I guess. She has problems finishing the simplest work. She keeps to herself on the playground."

Rachel fiddled with her purse strap. "Becky's been having nightmares since the tornado."

"I know she's good friends with Erin. Erin seems to be getting along remarkably well."

"Yes, I know. But Becky was over there that day, and the experience has frightened her beyond reason."

"Well, at least now I understand what is causing the change in her. I didn't know she was there when it happened." The teacher gave Rachel a helpless look. "Have you considered some kind of counseling?"

"Until now, no, but I'll certainly check into it." Standing, Rachel extended her hand to Kristin. "Thank you for bringing Becky's school problems to my attention."

As Rachel drove home, she contemplated Becky's need for counseling that wasn't available in their small town. Was taking Becky back to California the best solution? Getting her away from the constant reminder of the disaster seemed to be the only answer. But that decision meant saying good-bye to Matt. He couldn't leave, and she couldn't stay.

With a heavy heart, Rachel talked to Becky about going back to California. She listened quietly while Rachel explained the reasons they needed to leave. Becky made no protest even after learning she would have to leave her horse behind. Rachel was beginning to understand her daughter's fear of being separated from her. She only hoped she was making the right decision.

After talking with Becky, Rachel went to the Dalton farm where Matt was still working. What she had to say wasn't going to be easy, but there was no sense postponing it.

Nothing at the farm looked the same. The tornado had demolished the trees and shrubs that once surrounded the old farmhouse. The shell of the new house was on the other side of the drive. The house, the trees and fences could be replaced, but nothing could replace the budding relationship her declaration was about to shatter. But maybe this was God's way of sparing her heartache down the road.

After getting out of the car, Rachel skirted the construction material lying in the yard. Once inside the house, she saw Matt and John nailing drywall to the studs.

"Matt," she called, moving closer to where they worked.

He stopped hammering and turned, a smile spreading across his face. He walked over and gave her a peck on the cheek. "Hey, what brings you by?"

Her heart twisted in pain. How could she bring herself to wipe away that smile? "Can you take a few minutes to talk?"

"Anything for a beautiful lady." He put his hammer down. "Let's go outside."

Standing on the unpainted boards of the new porch, Rachel remembered being on the old porch and talking with Matt right after the funeral. It seemed ages ago. So many things had happened since then. Now she was going to destroy whatever could have been between Matt and her as quickly as the tornado had torn apart the old porch. She'd hoped they would find a middle ground, but she realized today it was an impossible dream.

"So what did you want?" he asked, interrupting her thoughts.

Rachel drew a deep breath. "I'm taking Becky back to California, and I'm not coming back."

He stared at her. "Ever?"

She saw him swallow hard. She didn't want to do this, but she didn't have a choice. "Not ever."

"Why?"

"I have to get Becky away from here. You know the terrible nightmares she's been having."

"But that doesn't mean you have to stay away forever. What about us?"

"There can't be an 'us.'" Turning away, she stared at the place where Sarah and John's house once stood. She didn't want to look into those golden eyes and see the hurt. She didn't want to cave in and change her mind. An iron hand squeezed her heart. She steeled herself against the pain.

"Yes, there can." He placed a hand on her shoulder and turned her to face him.

Shaking her head, she tried to ward off the sensations his touch aroused. Walking out of his life forever wasn't what she wanted to do, but she saw no other way. "Don't make this hard on me, Matt."

He laughed harshly. "Don't make this hard on you. How about me? How can you just walk away?"

"We can't live in two different worlds and expect things to work out." She turned away again. "Please accept it."

"I'm not accepting anything. Becky can get better. I know. I got better."

Rachel frowned. "What do you mean? Becky doesn't have the kind of injuries you suffered."

"Not the physical ones, but the mental ones. I think she might be suffering from post-traumatic stress disorder. I had the nightmares, too, but they were always about the explosion. Becky never dreamed about the tornado, but it seems similar."

"So you're telling me she has post-traumatic stress disorder? Like someone who's been in a war?"

"I don't know, but you can get her counseling. Take her back to California, but when she's better you can come back. I'll wait. I thought we were going to see how things could work out between us."

"No, Matt. I just don't see how we can ever work things out. This whole thing has made me see that our lives are on two different courses." She wanted to cry, but she called upon all of her acting talents to make it appear that she was quite comfortable with her decision.

"So you're telling me what we've shared is worth nothing to you." Hurt radiated from Matt's voice.

"I didn't say that." Why couldn't he understand the impossible odds of their relationship? This conversation was killing her. But the pain of ending the relationship now would save them greater anguish in the future. "I feel like I'm being asked to make a choice between you and Becky, you and my career."

His gaze narrowed. "I would never ask you to choose between me and anything. Didn't you hear what I said? Take care of Becky, but don't shut me out. Leave the door open for me, for us."

She surveyed his face. A light stubble covered his strong jaw. She pushed away the urge to kiss the frown from his lips. What he was asking wasn't unreasonable. But what was the sense in holding out false hope? They should end it here and save themselves future heartache. "I'm not going to make any promises I can't keep."

"I'm not asking you to make any promises. Just don't turn your back on me completely." His golden eyes searched her face. "I thought, after all these years, God had brought us together."

Rachel breathed deeply, then slowly released her breath. "Maybe God just wanted us together so I would turn my life back to Him."

Matt slowly nodded. "Yes, I believe He did that, but maybe there's more. Our shared faith can help us overcome the obstacles."

"How do you know?"

"I've been praying about it."

Shaking her head, Rachel closed her eyes to hold back the tears. Opening her eyes, she stared at him, her heart breaking. "I guess my faith isn't that strong."

"It can be," he said, stepping closer. "When you go away, pray about us and see what God reveals to you."

Rachel steeled herself against her weakening resolve. She

couldn't see a happy future for them. "Just for you, I will, but it won't change anything. It's over, Matt. Becky and I are leaving as soon as I can get a flight. This is good-bye." She turned to go.

Matt grabbed her arm. "I want you to remember this." He gave her a slow kiss.

Her head wanted to pull away, but her heart wanted to stay. There was no doubt she would remember how his kisses made her heart thunder and her knees weak. His kiss was a brand on her lips, an imprint on her heart, one she would never forget.

Chapter Fourteen

Rachel looked at Becky, absorbed in a movie on her portable DVD player in the backseat of Sarah's car. Even though Rachel believed she'd made the right decision, her heart ached because she didn't have what she wanted most. Matt's love.

Even when he'd tried to convince her to stay, he didn't say the words she wanted to hear. He never said he loved her. He'd always said he cared. Was he the kind of man who found it hard to say those three little words? What did it matter now? She was leaving.

Sarah reached across the console of her car and touched Rachel's arm. "I know it's been tough dealing with Becky's situation."

"I'm praying about it." Rachel put her hand over her heart. "Thank you for helping me find what was missing in my life for a long time. God helps when the bad times come. I didn't see that when my father died, but I see it now."

Sarah nodded. "I see the change in you."

Rachel chuckled. "I was thinking about you and how much you've helped me. I see how you've handled loss by relying on God."

"I know I promised not to mention you-know-who, but I'm going to be praying about that situation, too."

"It's an impossible—"

"Remember with God, all things are possible."

Sighing, Rachel gave Sarah a helpless smile but ignored her comment. "My Uncle Henry gave me the name of a pastor at a church near my home in California. I've already talked with him about enrolling Becky in their school. He's checking into a Christian counselor for her. I'm supposed to call him tomorrow."

"You're going to be one busy lady."

"You're the one who's going to be busy. I'm so sorry I have to leave you in the lurch with the theater."

"Don't worry about it. You gave us a good start. We learned a lot from you." Sarah pulled up to the terminal and helped Rachel unload her bags. After giving Becky and her a hug, Sarah grabbed something from the console. "Here's a good book to read on the plane. I think it would make a great movie."

"Thanks. This plane trip may be the last chance I have for pleasure reading. Once we get back, I won't have much time for it. Art already has things lined up for me." Rachel hugged Sarah and reminded herself that being busy wasn't all bad. It left little time to think about Matt. She had to leave him in the past and move on. She'd done it once before. She could do it again, but this time it wouldn't be as easy.

Matt sat in the den as he tried to read the local paper. He looked up to see John and Sarah watching something on TV while Erin worked on her homework at the kitchen table. They seemed content, but Matt felt restless in this house. Nearly three months had passed since Rachel had left, but everything here made him think of her. Wanting to leave these reminders behind, he longed for the day when they could move into their own place again. He returned his attention to the newspaper just as Erin came bounding into the room.

"I'm finished. Will you check my work?" She handed her papers to John.

He looked them over and handed them back. "Looks good to me."

"Can I check my e-mail now?"

"Yes," John replied with a chuckle. "What did they do before e-mail?"

"We wrote letters with pencil and paper," Sarah said. "Personally, I'm with Erin. E-mails are better."

"Does she get e-mail from Becky every day?" John asked.

"Just about." Sarah looked Matt's way.

He knew what that look was about. Why didn't she and John just come out and tell him what a fool he was? Instead, they hinted around the edges. Were they trying to make him more miserable than he already was? The way things were going even moving out of this house wasn't going to make forgetting Rachel any easier.

Laying the paper aside, he got up and went into the kitchen. He didn't want to see any conspiring looks or the happy domestic scene that John and Sarah presented. Living in the same house with them wasn't going to be as uncomplicated as he'd originally thought. Their happiness would be a constant reminder of the love he'd lost.

As Matt went to the cupboard to get a glass for a drink of water, he heard Sarah call out. "Erin, come and look. Rachel's on TV."

Matt nearly let the glass slip from his hand, but he tightened his grip at the last second. Taking a deep breath, he proceeded to fill the glass with water. This was something he didn't need. What was she doing on TV? She didn't have a show anymore. While he drank the water, Erin came running into the kitchen.

"Matt." She tugged on his arm. "You have to come watch."

Erin didn't know what had happened between him and Rachel and so believed she was doing him a favor. He might as well get used to seeing Rachel on TV and in the movies. Avoiding them for the rest of his life would be impossible. But did he want to put himself through this? At this point, he didn't have a choice as Erin dragged him into the den.

"What's she doing on this show?" John asked as Matt sat down.

"Talking about her new movie that's coming out right before Christmas. She's been working with a group who plans to make movies with messages of hope and faith," Sarah said. "And she's promoting the foundation she started when the tornado hit here. Isn't this exciting?"

"You've seen her on TV hundreds of times before." John talked to Sarah, but looked pointedly at Matt.

"But I didn't know her then."

"You get too excited, but I love that about you." John chuckled and hugged Sarah's shoulders as he gave her a peck on the cheek.

Matt glowered at the TV. What was John trying to do? Show off because the woman he loved was sitting beside him while the woman Matt loved was on TV half a continent away. And all because he'd failed to tell her he loved her.

Matt didn't want to watch or listen, but he couldn't help himself. His heart ached as he heard her voice. She talked about her experiences here on the farm and how it had changed her outlook on life. He closed his eyes.

"Are you praying, Matt?" Erin asked as a commercial came on.

Quickly opening his eyes, he shook his head. "No. I'm just tired." He was tired of kidding himself, tired of pretending losing Rachel didn't matter. He should be praying. He'd told

Rachel to pray, but he'd let his own prayer life falter. Could God undo the mess he'd made, or would He in His wisdom use Matt's mistake for some greater purpose?

"Rachel's back on," Erin announced as the camera zoomed in for a close-up shot, then zoomed out to include the interviewer. "I wonder if Becky ever gets to be on TV. I'm going to e-mail her right now and ask, and I'll say I saw her mom on TV."

While Erin went back to her room, Matt listened to the interview despite himself. The reporter asked her about the fundraiser she'd started, first for the tornado victims here and then for the recent earthquake victims out in California. She told them about the foundation that helped others in a time of tragedy.

Matt remembered the day Henry Charbonneau had come to the house with their check. Calling John aside, Henry talked with John at length, then gave him the check. After Henry left, John shouted and jumped up and down like a kid, running around the farmyard and waving the check in the air. When he finally calmed down and showed Matt, he understood John's behavior. The amount read ten thousand dollars.

Matt learned then of Rachel's fundraiser and foundation. His only thought was that she would rather give him her money than her love. The notion made him ache inside. He wanted to get up and leave, but he didn't want to hear from John if he did.

"She looks happy, doesn't she, Matt?" John asked.

"I guess if you can tell how happy someone is by the way they look on TV." Matt knew John was trying to get under his skin. He was reminding Matt in a subtle way not to let her go again. John wanted Matt to admit he'd been wrong to let her walk out of his life. Ever since that confrontation after the tornado, there was an uneasy tension between them.

"Well, we know one thing for sure. You're not happy."

"Who says?"

John laughed halfheartedly. "Nobody has to say. It's obvious."

"Quiet, you guys, I'm trying to listen to this," Sarah said. "She's talking about that book I gave her to read when she left."

"What about it?" John asked.

"She wants to make it into a movie." Sarah sat forward on the sofa and listened intently while Rachel told the interviewer how excited she was about her next project. When the interview was over and a commercial came on, Sarah looked at John. "I loved that story. It'll make such a great movie, and besides that, it has a Christian message. What a wonderful way to witness for the Lord."

Leaning back and stretching his legs out in front of him, Matt took in Sarah's comments. Despite what John said, maybe all God had ever planned was for Matt and Rachel to rekindle their friendship in order to bring her back to her faith. Now she was doing God's work in a way that would reach thousands of people. He could point that out to John, but Matt didn't want to argue any more.

"You know what you need, Matt?" Sarah asked.

"I'm afraid to ask."

"You need a date. And I have someone perfect in mind."

Sitting up, Matt held up his hands. "Please spare me any more of your matchmaking. Your last attempt ended badly."

"And whose fault was that?"

"No one's."

"Okay, I won't argue with you, but you can't sit around and mope for the rest of your life." Sarah stood. "I'm going to get Erin ready for bed."

Watching Sarah leave the room, Matt wanted to call after her. *Good. I'm glad you're going to mind your own business.* But he held his tongue. He didn't need to be at odds with both Sarah and John.

"You know she's right."

Matt turned in John's direction. Praying for strength, Matt resisted the urge to punch his cousin right in the nose. "Why do you two keep giving me advice when I don't want it?"

"Because we care about you. We don't like to see you unhappy."

"If you don't like to see me unhappy, then quit giving me advice." Matt glared at John.

John smiled. "Did you ever tell her you loved her? Did you say those three important words?"

"That's none of your business." Matt got up and went to look out the window. The yard light illuminated a blanket of snow that covered everything in sight. The cattle were in the feedlots, the new house was almost finished and the farm was on good financial ground again. Christmas was barely two weeks away. It was a time for joy, but his heart wasn't joyful.

"You didn't. I thought not." John followed Matt and stood beside him. "Do you remember when I complained about Rachel not coming back here until her mother died?"

"Yeah. Why?"

"When I said that, you told me Rachel said her mother never expressed her wishes. Rachel said she would've come if she'd known. Maybe if you'd told her you loved and that you wanted her to stay she would've."

"No," Matt said, shaking his head. "She said she wasn't coming back. There was no hope for us."

"Things might have been different if you'd said those three little words. I love you."

"I doubt it." Matt had said those words to Amy, and in the end, it hadn't meant a thing. He was afraid to say them again.

"Mom, here's my letter to Santa." Becky handed a paper to Rachel. "Will you get an envelope for it?"

"May I read it first? Or is this private?"

"You can read it. Just don't forget to mail it. Now I'm going to send Erin a Christmas card."

"You mean you're not going to e-mail it?"

"I did one of those, too, but I want to send her a real card."

Rachel watched Becky skip back to her bedroom before she looked down at the paper in her hand. Smiling, Rachel read over the list to discover whether it contained anything she wasn't aware of. Everything looked familiar until Rachel got to the last item.

"A dad. This is what I want most."

Laying the letter aside, she sighed heavily. Was Matt still the prime candidate for the position?

There hadn't been a day since she'd left the farm that she hadn't thought of Matt, missed Matt, wanted Matt. She hadn't guessed how being without him would weigh on her heart and mind. She'd tried to push those thoughts aside, but she could never forget Matt's challenge for her to pray about their relationship.

Even though she prayed, she still didn't have an answer. That was the hard part about being a Christian. Sometimes, the answers weren't always clear.

Rachel talked with Sarah regularly on the phone and through e-mail, but they never talked about Matt. Rachel made it quite clear the first time Sarah mentioned him that she didn't want to talk about him. Sarah had obliged.

Rachel wanted to make the break complete. She believed it would be easier that way, but it wasn't. Now she was afraid to ask about him, fearful that he'd moved on and found someone else. She was reliving the past.

Rachel's professional life was at its zenith. Her return to California had brought with it the opportunity to make family-friendly movies with a small independent company. Now she had the opportunity to produce her own film, one that would send a message about God's love. She should have been thrilled, but something was missing.

Matt.

In the weeks since she'd returned to California, Rachel thought of Matt more than she cared to admit. She missed the farm, Sarah, John and Erin. Southern California was warm this time of year, but Rachel's heart was cold with wanting what she'd left behind. Was God telling her she'd made a mistake?

With the letter in hand, Rachel went to her desk and got out envelopes and stamps. Then she went into Becky's room. Becky wasn't there. As Rachel turned to go, she noticed the computer screen. Becky's e-mail program was still running. Sighing, Rachel started to close the program when she caught sight of the words on the screen.

becky we got to do something. my mom invited miss weiss to go to the movies with matt. We have to get your mom and matt back together. Then you can come here to live again.

Rachel's heart sank. Had Matt found someone else? Or was this some kind of plan Becky had cooked up to go along with her letter to Santa? Was the letter Becky's way of trying to get them back together? Rachel decided to find out.

"Becky," Rachel called as she walked through the house. She found Becky watching TV in the den. "Here's your letter to Santa, ready for the mail."

"Thanks, Mom."

Rachel walked across the room and sat down beside Becky. "I want to ask you something."

"What?"

"How do you think Santa can bring you a dad?"

Becky shrugged silently and kept watching TV.

"It's not really something Santa can do," Rachel said when Becky remained silent.

"I know. Santa's only make-believe, but I let you know how I feel. God can make it come true. I've been praying."

"I know. I've been praying, too." Rachel nodded, thinking about this special time of year when God's love was evident.

"Before we left the farm, I wanted Matt to be my dad, but I don't guess he thinks about us anymore. He never talks to us when I call Erin." Becky's solemn expression tore at Rachel's heart.

She never realized Becky's reaction to having Matt out of their lives. Rachel wondered how she could possibly explain that Matt hadn't turned his back on them. Instead, her own mother had turned her back on Matt.

"Matt still cares about us," Rachel said, wondering if it could be possible after the way she'd shut him out. "He's probably been very busy working on their house."

"Mom?" Becky turned Rachel's way. "Can we go see Erin and Matt when we're at Grandma and Grandpa's for Christmas?"

Rachel studied her daughter. Was this Becky's plan? Were her fears over? She had appeared to be fine for weeks. The nightmares were gone. The counselor she'd been seeing said there was no need for more sessions. Even the recent earthquake hadn't bothered her, and Rachel realized no matter where one lived disasters could strike. Safety only came from believing in God's promises.

Still, Rachel went to bed each night wondering whether she would be awakened by Becky's screams. Would taking her back to South Dakota and reminders of the tornado reawaken her fears?

"Are you sure you want to go back?"

Becky nodded vigorously. "I want to see Erin's new house."

"Are you afraid of having nightmares again?"

"No," Becky said, shaking her head. "I miss everything on the farm. Can we go back?"

Rachel nodded. "I think that's a good idea."

Becky jumped up and hugged Rachel. "I'm going to e-mail Erin."

Rachel grabbed Becky's shoulder. "Not so fast. I think we should make it a surprise."

"But I want you and Matt to get married because I want him to be my dad."

"Now that's *not* a surprise. I kind of figured that out from your Santa letter, but don't get your hopes up."

"But you love him, don't you, Mom?"

"Yes, I do."

"Then why didn't you get married before?"

Rachel contemplated the question. How could she answer? Becky wouldn't understand Rachel's reasons for walking away. Now she wondered whether Matt still cared, even though she'd told Becky he did. Marrying Matt might mean putting an end to her career, but Becky's happiness and her own meant more. "The time wasn't right."

"Is the time right now?"

"I think so," Rachel said, seeing God's guidance in her daughter's words. *Yes, I think so if I'm not too late.*

Big fluffy snowflakes fell from the sky as Matt exited the theater beside Kristin Weiss. White blanketed the streets, sidewalks and cars. The streetlights made the falling snow glitter in the darkness. John, Sarah and Erin walked ahead of them, leaving footprints in the newly fallen snow.

When they reached their car, John looked at Sarah. "No more shopping. If we leave now, we should get home before there's too much accumulation."

"That's okay." Sarah opened the car door. "I got most of my shopping done before the movie."

"Are you glad I convinced you to see this movie?" Sarah asked Matt as they settled in the car.

"Yes. Rachel's good, very good," he replied.

"Did you enjoy it, Kristin?" Sarah asked.

"Yes, and it was so cool having actually met her. On one of those entertainment-magazine TV shows, some of the critics said they think she'll get an Academy Award nomination," Kristin replied, smiling at Matt. "How's Becky doing?"

"Ask Sarah," Matt replied. "She's the local grapevine."

"Becky's doing great," Sarah said. "She and Erin e-mail every day."

"I'm glad. I hated to see them leave."

"Me, too," Sarah added. "I had no idea how good the movie would be when Rachel told me about it."

"Me, neither," John said as he drove toward the interstate.

Matt listened to the conversation buzz around him. All he could think about was Rachel. He didn't want to be here with Kristin. He wanted to be with Rachel, but he couldn't very well be rude. After all, it wasn't Kristin's fault that Sarah kept trying to get them together, inviting Kristin to Sunday dinner last week and now on this shopping trip into Sioux Falls. Then to top it all off, Sarah insisted that they go to Rachel's movie. Was Sarah trying to torture him?

Throughout the rest of the ride home, Matt tried to keep up his end of the conversation, but Rachel was never far from his thoughts. The movie played through his mind. The story made an impact with its message of hope. It told him he'd been a coward. He'd let her go. He was every kind of fool, just like the hero in the movie. But in the movie, the hero had come to his senses and won Rachel's heart. Now Matt planned to do the same thing for real.

When they arrived home, Matt stopped Sarah as they walked into the house. "Sarah, I'm putting an end to your matchmaking."

She looked at him with fake indignation. "My matchmaking?

"How's that?"

"I've made up my mind. Now that the house is done, I'm going to L.A. and do whatever it takes to convince Rachel to marry me."

"What?" Sarah placed her hand over her heart. "You two haven't spoken in months. What's she going to say?"

"Yes, I hope."

"This is incredible. Did going out with someone else make you realize how much you missed Rachel?"

"No. The movie made me realize I'd given up too easily."

"When do you plan to do this?" Sarah asked.

"As soon as school's out, I'm catching the first flight I can get."

Sarah looked at Matt. "You can't do that."

"Why? I'll sell my horse or my pickup if that's what it takes to get a ticket. I don't care what it costs. Somehow, I'm going to get there."

"Going to L.A. would be a big mistake because—"

"Don't try to tell me I can't. I won't take no for an answer. I did that once before, but not this time."

"If you'd let me finish, I'm trying to tell you Rachel won't be in L.A. for Christmas. She's going to Rapid to see her grandparents."

"How do you know? How come you didn't tell me?"

"I know because I talked with her last week, and I didn't tell you because you never asked."

Matt glanced at Sarah with a wry smile. "I didn't ask because I thought that's the way she wanted it."

"Well, I don't think either of you was thinking very clearly," Sarah said. "I understand why Rachel had to take Becky away from here for a while, but I couldn't figure out why it had to be so permanent. And you let her go."

"What was I supposed to do? She was very clear about not wanting some man trying to run her life."

"That kept you from telling her you loved her?" John asked.

Matt nodded. "I know you've been wanting to hear this, John. Okay, here it is. You were right, and I was wrong."

John came over and put a hand on Matt's shoulder. "I just wanted you to do the right thing. Tell her you love her."

"That's what I intend to do. But that might mean you won't have me to help with the farm. Can you guys do without me?"

"If that's what makes you happy." John clapped Matt on the back.

"Then it looks like I'm going to Rapid City."

Chapter Fifteen

Rachel slowly awakened as the sun sent a sliver of light around the window shade. Looking about the room, she smiled, remembering where she was.

On the farm.

She'd never guessed how good it would feel to be here with Becky and her grandparents. She worried how Becky would react coming back, but she went to her own room with no problem other than wanting to call Erin. Rachel had persuaded Becky to wait until morning because it was so late.

Rachel was eager to see Matt, but what kind of reception would she get? After going into the kitchen to make coffee, she realized she needed to make a trip to the grocery. Hurriedly, she made a list, then headed for the store. As she maneuvered the car up the snow-covered lane, she thought about Matt. If she were a brave woman she would head right for the Dalton farm and beg Matt to forgive her foolishness. But she needed more time to summon the courage to admit her mistake and ask him to take her back.

Before Rachel reached the main road, a pickup turned in, blocking her exit. When she realized the driver was Sarah, she jumped from her car and ran across the packed snow to greet Sarah. They hugged and laughed like a couple of schoolgirls.

"What are you doing here?" Sarah asked when they finally calmed down. "When did you get here?"

"Late last night. We've come for Christmas. Becky and my grandparents are with me." Rachel beamed. "I came to see Matt and tell him I was wrong. Do you think there's any chance he'll listen and forgive me?"

"Matt," Sarah blurted and then put her gloved hand to the side of her face. "Oh no. Matt."

"Is something wrong with Matt?" Rachel asked. Her imagination ran wild with terrible possibilities. Maybe he was serious about Becky's former teacher and had decided to marry her. Rachel wondered whether she'd realized her mistake too late.

"No," Sarah said with a helpless laugh. "He left over an hour ago on his way to Rapid City to see you."

"He's going to Rapid to see me? Why?"

"Why do you suppose? Because he's crazy in love with you, and like you, he's finally come to his senses." Sarah started to laugh. "And you're here to see him. Oh, this is so funny, but it's not."

"We've got to stop him."

Sarah looked thoughtful. "He has his cell phone with him, but I'm not sure whether he can get a signal out there. He might not even have it on."

"We can try." Rachel headed back to her car.

Both women hurried into the kitchen where Sarah immediately grabbed the phone and punched in Matt's number. With the phone still to her ear, Sarah shook her head. "No answer. It went straight to voice mail."

"Now what?"

"I'll call John. See what he thinks." She punched in the

number. "Luckily, when we built the new house, we ran a phone line to the barn, so if he's out there he'll still answer," she explained as she waited.

Before Rachel could comment, Sarah began talking with John. She explained what had happened. Rachel stood by, hoping he could provide some answers.

After Sarah hung up, Rachel asked, "What did he say?"

"He's going to make some calls, then get back with us." Sarah sat at the kitchen table.

"I hope he can do something." Rachel joined Sarah.

"What'll happen if we don't stop him?"

"He'll be smart enough to turn around and come back home. He'll want to wring my neck because I told him you were in Rapid. But hopefully when he sees you, he'll forget all about killing me." Sarah chuckled.

Rachel turned at the sound of Becky's voice. "Mom, where's Erin? I want to see her."

"Hi, Becky," Sarah said. "Erin will come over with her dad. She's visiting with her grandparents, too." Turning to Rachel, Sarah added, "John's parents are here. And Paul and Jim and their families are coming this afternoon."

"It'll be good to see them again."

Grandpa Hofer entered the kitchen. "What's all the commotion?"

Rachel quickly filled in her grandparents and Becky on the events of the morning.

"Well, someone should get groceries. So while all of you are waiting on news about Matt, I'll head to town." Grandpa got his coat and took the shopping list.

"Sarah!" Rachel looked her friend over from head to toe. "With all the excitement, I didn't notice how much weight you've lost. You look great."

"Thanks. I figured after I'd lost almost all of my clothes in the storm that if I got a new wardrobe, it was going to fit a slimmer me."

"Why didn't you tell me how well you were doing?"

"I was afraid if I talked about it, I wouldn't stick with it." Sarah grinned sheepishly.

A knock at the door made Rachel jump from her chair to answer it. John came in followed by Erin. Becky and Erin raced to hug each other and squealed with delight just as their mothers had done earlier.

John removed his cap. "I've found a solution to your problem. I called the sheriff's department, and Steve contacted this guy in Mitchell who has a helicopter he uses to air spray crops. They've used him before to track people."

"Is he willing to do this on Christmas Eve?" Rachel asked.

"Probably, if the price is right." John handed Rachel a piece of paper. "But before you call him, try Matt one more time."

Rachel called Matt again without success. With a knot in her stomach, Rachel called the helicopter pilot. When the man answered, she explained the situation and smiled when he agreed to find Matt. She turned to John and handed him the phone. "He needs a description of Matt's pickup and the license plate number."

Hanging up, John looked at Rachel. "It'll take him at least two hours to catch up with Matt. Maybe more, depending on how far he's driven."

"I hope he wasn't speeding." Sarah laughed.

An hour later, Grandpa Hofer returned with a carload of groceries. Rachel, Sarah and the girls helped bring them in and put everything away.

"Do you still have a Christmas Eve open house like John's folks used to?" Rachel asked as she put away the last of the canned goods.

"Yeah."

"I loved going over there on Christmas Eve. Going to the Daltons was as much a part of Christmas Eve as going to church. Santa always came to their house. Does he still?" Rachel asked, winking at Sarah.

"He sure does. The kids love it. With Paul and Jim's families, there's always a crowd." Sarah peered at Rachel. "I'm so glad you came, Rachel. Now you and Matt can finally be together. This is going to be a great Christmas."

"I hope you're right."

"Are you worried Matt won't be glad to see you?"

"A little."

"How could you be? The man left the rest of us behind to be with you. He might be angry about the extra miles he's driven today, but he'll be happy to see you."

Rachel smiled. "This seems like a dream. I was so afraid he'd never forgive me. I was thinking only of myself."

"You had Becky to think about."

"Yes, but that didn't mean I should shut Matt out."

"Will you quit pacing?" Sarah grinned. "You're going to wear a hole in the floor."

"I can't help it. I wish someone would let us know if that helicopter pilot has found Matt. The wait is killing me."

"I'm sure we'll find out soon. Let's take the kids sledding. The time will go faster that way."

"All right!" Erin grabbed Becky's hand. "We can go down by the pond. It's frozen. Come on, Becky."

"That was a vote from the kids. What about you, Rachel?"

"I suppose you're right. It's better than sitting here wondering and waiting. But what if someone calls?"

"Take your cell phone. You can even try Matt's phone from time to time. Your grandparents are here, and John will be near a phone at our place."

"Okay, you've convinced me," Rachel said.

* * *

Matt sped down the interstate while snow-covered fields glistened in the morning light. The temperature was cold, but thoughts of seeing Rachel and Becky warmed his heart. Brightly wrapped gifts filled the seat next to him in the pickup. He had to convince Rachel to marry him. He would move to California if that was what it took.

Matt passed numerous cars carrying holiday travelers. He didn't want to get picked up for speeding, but whenever he glanced at the speedometer, he was going over the limit. He figured the trip would take him about five hours if he drove straight through.

As Matt neared Murdo, signs advertising the 1880 Town reminded him of last summer's trip and how Becky had begged to stop. Retracing the route of that memorable trip made him wonder how he'd ever thought he could remove Rachel and Becky from his life.

Suddenly, the steady thub, thub, thub of helicopter blades disturbed his thoughts. His brow knit in a puzzled frown as he realized a chopper pilot was practically sitting on top of his pickup. What was this guy trying to do? Where had he come from? Tourists took helicopter riders during the summer, but this was the dead of winter. Matt tried speeding up and then slowing down. The chopper stayed right with him. The guy was flying almost in his face, then alongside him.

Matt watched as the pilot held up a sign reading STOP EMERGENCY. What was going on? Someone must have sent this guy after him. Matt pulled to the side of the road and stopped. The helicopter sped on ahead and then turned back and landed in the adjacent field. The chopper blades kicked up a cloud of snow before slowing enough to allow the pilot to exit and trot across the field toward Matt's pickup.

When the man drew near, Matt rolled down the window and asked, "What's the emergency?"

"You Matt Dalton?" the man asked.

"Yeah."

"Your local sheriff contacted me to find you and tell you you're to go back home."

"Why? What's wrong?" Matt asked.

"Hey, I'm sorry. They didn't tell me anything. Just to get you back home." The man shook his head apologetically. "I can fly you back if you want to find a place to park your pickup."

Matt debated for a moment. Days could pass before he could get back. A storm might develop. "No, I don't feel comfortable leaving it out here. As long as this isn't a life-and-death situation, I'll drive back."

"I can't say for sure, but my guess is that it's not. They usually let me know in cases like that."

"I hope you're right. Thanks," Matt said, starting his pickup again. He waved as the pilot ran for his chopper.

Worried, anxious, and a little miffed, Matt drove to the next exit and turned around and headed east on the interstate. The helicopter flew ahead of him. Why hadn't anyone bothered to let him know what this emergency was all about? He contemplated several scenarios. Maybe John had had an accident with some machinery. He forced himself to quit guessing. Thinking about the possibilities was doing him no good. He wondered whether he'd ever get to be with Rachel.

As he drove, he pulled out his cell phone to see whether he could get a signal. Nothing. He left the phone on and checked every few minutes. Finally a couple of bars appeared on the screen. He slowed his pickup and pulled over to the side. He punched in John and Sarah's number. The phone rang several times until the answering machine picked up. When he was about to end the call, a female voice sounded over the message on the machine.

"Sarah?"

"No, this is Lisa. Who's this?"

"Matt. What's going on there?"

"Paul and I and the kids just got here, and everything's chaos. They're taking Erin to the hospital. We'll fill you in when you get home—"

"Lisa, Lisa." The line went dead. No signal again. He sighed. This sounded more serious than that chopper pilot had indicated. Erin must've been in an accident. Why were they just now taking her to the hospital? Matt pulled back onto the highway and tried not to speed despite his eagerness to return home.

When Matt finally pulled into the drive at the farm, he recognized Paul and Lisa's car parked near the house. In the dusky light of early evening, the Christmas tree lights shone through the front window. Part of him was glad he'd spend Christmas here, but mostly he was disappointed not to be with Rachel. Jogging toward the house, he hoped, whatever the emergency, it wouldn't put a damper on the holiday celebration.

Matt walked into the kitchen. Paul and Lisa were in the dining room setting out paper plates, napkins, and plastic cups on the table. Their three boys were chasing each other through the house. Matt grabbed one by the arm.

"Hey, Matt," the boy cried.

Matt saw Paul and Lisa turn at the sound of their son's voice. Matt walked into the dining room. "What's happening?"

"When we walked in the door, John was going to Sioux Falls to pick up Jim and Mary and their kids at the airport. Sarah and everyone else had already left to take Erin to the hospital because she broke her arm," Paul said. "They put us in charge of getting things ready for tonight. They're still planning to have the party."

Matt wrinkled his brow. "They didn't say how it happened or how bad it was?"

"No, but it couldn't be that bad if they're going ahead with their plans." Paul continued the party preparations. "Where have you been?"

Matt explained to Paul and then added, "I'm sorry Erin broke her arm, but it puzzles me that they brought me back because of that."

"We'll know soon enough. Just before you came in John called and said they're minutes away and the others are coming home from the hospital." Paul started working again.

"So they took Erin to the hospital here?" Matt asked, lending a hand.

"I guess. We'll learn all the details when everyone gets back."

Muttering to himself, Matt drove the pickup to Rachel's house. His irritation had finally gotten the best of him when Sarah asked him to retrieve Erin's gifts. He was furious with Sarah for chasing after him and making him think he had to come home. Maybe she was trying to keep him from seeing Rachel.

The headlights of an oncoming car shook him from his reverie. Probably someone headed to the open house. Turning into the drive, he figured he might as well spend some time at the empty house to cool his temper and get into the holiday spirit.

Rachel heard the key in the lock. Her heart thundered as she sat in the darkened den. She didn't know what to do. Should she just wait for Matt to come in and turn on the light? Should she run to greet him? What would she say to him? If she called to him out of the darkness, she might scare him. Why had she let Sarah talk her into this crazy scheme? Wouldn't it have been easier to go over to the Daltons' and say, "Here I am. I love you."

The light came on in the kitchen, casting a beam through the door into the den. Tightness formed in her throat, and an awkward feeling swept over her as she sat there. When she saw his figure silhouetted in the doorway, she stood up. Swallowing the lump in her throat, she took a step forward. "Matt."

His head jerked in her direction as the hand he'd lifted to turn on the light fell to his side. "Who's there?"

Disappointment flooded her mind when he didn't recognize her. Somehow she'd imagined that he'd know the sound of her voice and race across the room to scoop her up in his arms. Maybe she'd read too many movie scripts. She reached for the lamp next to the couch and fumbled with the switch. He squinted against the light until his eyes adjusted. He stood there with his mouth hanging open.

"Hi, it's me," she said, feeling suddenly shy.

A big grin spread across his face. He hurried across the room and grabbed her around the waist. Laughing, crying and sighing all at once, she melted into his arms. His embrace crushed her. His mouth found hers. How she had missed his lips, his strong arms, everything about him.

When Rachel thought her knees would give out, Matt pulled back, gazing into her eyes. "How did you get here?"

"Santa brought me."

Matt chuckled. "Santa's a good man. Did Sarah know you were over here?"

Nodding, Rachel smiled. "But not until this morning. Then she told me you were on your way to Rapid. When we couldn't get you on your cell phone, we sent the helicopter after you." She pulled him down to sit next to her on the couch. "Then Erin broke her arm while we were sledding, and everything went crazy around here. We were trying to juggle taking Erin to the doctor, then to the hospital for X-rays, picking up John's brother at the airport and getting back in time for the open house."

Gazing into his golden eyes, she wondered what he was thinking. "And all the time I was wondering if you'd forgive me for the way I shut you out. I was wrong."

"Hold on. I'll be back in a minute." He kissed her soundly on the lips and then sprinted from the room, despite his limp.

When Matt returned, he found Rachel standing in the middle of the kitchen. Her eyes studied him. Taking her hand, he led her back into the den and sat with her on the couch. He'd rehearsed his speech in his head while he'd been driving, but now his mind was blank.

"You didn't answer my question. Do you forgive me?" She gazed at him, her eyes wide with anxiety.

"I forgive you, if you can forgive me for never telling you how much you mean to me." His heart pounding, he had to say those three little words. "Rachel, I love you. Marry me. I'll move to California tomorrow if that's what it takes to win your heart."

Rachel shook her head. "No, Matt, you—"

The resounding "no" stabbed his heart. Had she come all this way to ask his forgiveness and then slam the door in his face again? It didn't make sense. "Why did you come here, Rachel, if you don't want to marry me?"

"No, Matt," she nearly cried. "I didn't mean *no I won't marry you.* I mean you don't have to move to California." She threw her arms around him. "Yes, I'll marry you. Becky and I will move here. We can live in this house."

He held her at arms' length. "Is Becky okay with living here? Is she over the nightmares?"

Rachel nodded. "She'll be all right. She's the one who wanted to come back. You can thank her for making me see how foolish I've been. She wanted a dad for Christmas, and I plan to give her one."

"You aren't marrying me just to give Becky a dad, are you?"

"No, I'm marrying you because I love you and I don't want to live without you in my life. God used a little girl to help me see what was right."

"He does have a way of working things out when we trust Him." Matt took her hands in his. "What about your career?"

"I'm going to trust God to work that out, too. I'm going to work on projects that are family-friendly. We need more movies like that. God can use me to send His message." Rachel hugged Matt. "But whatever I do, I won't let it interfere with my family."

Matt reached in his pocket and brought out a small box and flipped it open. The diamond ring sparkled like twinkling Christmas lights. "Let's make it official," he said, offering her the ring.

Rachel extended her left hand, and he placed the ring on her finger. "Shall we seal it with a kiss?"

He answered by pulling her into his arms and giving her another kiss.

"Hey, anybody here?" Matt and Rachel jerked apart at the sound of the voice.

Standing, Matt peered toward the kitchen. "We're in here."

A large man in a Santa suit came into the den. Bells jingled as he walked. She leaned over and whispered in Matt's ear. "And here I thought your kisses were making me hear bells."

"Sarah sent me over here to get you two. She thought you'd like to be there when Santa arrives," the Santa said.

Rachel turned to Matt. "Who is this?"

"Rachel, meet Santa. Santa, meet Rachel."

"Come on, Matt."

"I'm serious. This guy is Santa. He shows up every year on Christmas Eve."

Rachel looked more closely. "The hair and beard are real.

So maybe there is a Santa. Who am I to question Santa on the best Christmas ever?" Rachel pushed Matt forward. "Well, Santa, my little girl Becky wants a dad for Christmas, and I'd like you to bring her one. Can you wrap him up?"

"Let's see what we can do," Santa said with a grin.

Rachel walked into the new house. The smell of baking mingled with that of new construction. Laughter, lights and love warmed the house.

When Sarah saw Rachel, she came immediately to her side. "Where's Matt? Did everything work out?" Sarah asked, concern knitting her brow.

Rachel nodded with a smile and whispered in Sarah's ear when she saw Becky approaching. Sarah nodded and smiled back.

"Mom, where's Matt?"

Before Rachel could answer, John let out a sharp whistle that quieted the crowd. "Good. I've got everyone's attention. Because of our crazy day most of us didn't have a chance to attend the Christmas Eve service at church. So before we start the evening's festivities we're going to take some time to recognize the real reason for our celebration."

Becky tugged on Rachel's arm and whispered, "Mom, you didn't answer my question."

Rachel put a finger to her lips. "I'll tell you when John is done. You can go up there to the front with the other kids and listen to what he has to say."

Becky reluctantly joined the other children gathered near the Christmas tree while John picked up his Bible. Soon John's voice filled the room with the Christmas story, first from the gospel of Matthew, then from the gospel of Luke. After he finished reading, the group sang several Christmas carols. Finally, he said a prayer asking God to bless all those gathered for this time of celebration.

When John finished, Becky scrambled to her feet, but before she reached her mother, John called out, "Hey, kids, Santa's here."

The children quickly gathered around John. Squeals of delight filled the living room as the large bearded man stepped through the door. Looking over the children, he said, "Is there a little girl named Becky here?"

She waved her arms above her head. "I'm Becky!"

"Well, come right over here, young lady."

Becky made her way through the other children until she was standing next to Santa. "Hi, Santa."

"I've heard that you've been an especially good girl. So I've brought you something you've been wanting for a long time."

Becky looked around. "Where is it?"

"Right near the back door in the kitchen."

Becky, followed by the other children, ran into the kitchen. Rachel observed as Becky stopped in front of a large box with a big red ribbon tied around it.

"Here, you can cut the ribbon with this." She handed Becky a pair of scissors.

Becky pulled Rachel down and whispered, "Mom, it has a picture of a refrigerator on the box. I didn't ask for that."

Straightening, Rachel laughed. "Go ahead. Open it. You won't be disappointed."

Becky walked over to the box and cut the ribbon. It fell to the floor. Rachel nodded for Becky to open the door cut in the side. Tightness filled Rachel's chest as she watched Becky open the door to find Matt standing inside.

"Matt!" Becky grinned from ear to ear. "Are you my Christmas present?"

"I sure am. I hope you don't want to exchange me." He stepped from the box and picked her up. "Tell your mom to come over here."

"Mom," Becky called.

When Rachel was standing next to Matt, he reached down and grabbed her left hand. "You see this on your mom's finger? Your mom said she'd marry me. Santa told me you wanted a dad. Do you think I'll do?"

Smiling, Becky gave Matt a big hug. "Yeah. I *told* Mom she should marry you. This is going to be the best Christmas ever. This is like coming home."

"Yes, it is, Becky. We're finally coming home for good."

* * * * *

Dear Reader,

Thank you for reading *Mommy's Hometown Hero*. I hope you enjoyed reading it as much as I enjoyed writing it. This story is dear to my heart because it is set in South Dakota where I was born and lived several different times in my early years, the last time when I was in college. Writing this story brought as many fond memories to me as it did to my heroine, Rachel.

I hope Rachel's return to her hometown and the renewal of her faith will remind you of God's patience with us when we lose sight of His promise to be with us in all circumstances. God is there even when we don't feel His presence. He is there ready to keep His promises. We just have to turn our lives over to Him.

I love to hear from readers. You can write to me at P.O. Box 16461, Fernandina Beach, Florida 32035, or through my Web site, www.merrilleewhren.com.

May God bless you,

Merrillee Whren

QUESTIONS FOR DISCUSSION

1. Why does Rachel hate the farm where she grew up? Has there ever been a place you disliked because it revived bad memories? How did you deal with it?

2. Rachel hasn't seen Matt for many years and isn't sure how to relate to him. Has there ever been a time when you didn't know what to say to someone you hadn't seen for a long time? What did you do to break the ice?

3. Rachel feels that God turned His back on her when her father died. How might John 11:25,26 help someone who has lost someone they love?

4. In the story, many people have been praying for Rachel through the years. When Rachel expresses her doubt about the effectiveness of prayers, what does her grandmother tell her? What scripture does her grandmother reference? Discuss a time when you may have questioned whether God answers prayer.

5. Matt wants Rachel to stay, but he isn't sure how to persuade her to make that decision. Have you ever wished that someone you cared about would follow your advice? How did you handle the situation?

6. During the story Rachel and Sarah become good friends. But when they first meet, they are unsure of each other. Discuss a time when your first impression of someone changed because you got to know that person better. Have

you ever become good friends with someone you didn't like at first? If so, what changed your mind?

7. Even though Rachel has pushed her faith far, far away, she remembers biblical teachings from her childhood. Although Rachel has doubts, she reminds Sarah that Christians should rely on God for their strength. Has God ever used a doubter or unbeliever to remind you of biblical teachings? How did you respond? Can you give an example from the Bible where God used unbelievers for His purpose?

8. Matt gives Becky kittens for her birthday. How does Rachel respond? Discuss the pros and cons of children having pets.

9. Rachel buys Becky a horse for her birthday, but she has second thoughts about her purchase when she sees Becky riding the horse. Why do you think she isn't sure about her choice? Discuss a time that you may have had second thoughts about a choice you have made.

10. Throughout the story Becky is eager to pray. How does Rachel feel about Becky's desire to pray? What is Rachel's reaction when Becky prays for a dad? What does Mark 11:24 say about prayer?

11. Why does Matt's mother warn Rachel away from Matt? Have you ever received some unwanted advice? If so, how did you react? What Christian principles can you apply when it comes to giving and receiving advice?

12. Sarah is reluctant to let anyone know that she is trying to

lose weight, because she is afraid she won't be success-ful. Discuss a time when you kept a goal to yourself because you feared failure. How can Philippians 4:13 relate to our goals?

13. What incident causes Rachel to turn to God? Has there ever been a time in your life when a traumatic experience has made you rely on God?

14. Rachel believes her relationship with Matt is impossible because their lives are on conflicting courses. What brings her to that conclusion? What does Matt ask her to do concerning their relationship?

15. Rachel and Matt are both willing to give up their way of life in order to be with each other. How does this change in their attitudes bring them together?

Love Inspired.
HISTORICAL

*Powerful, engaging stories of romance, adventure
and faith set in the past—when things were simpler
and faith played a major role in everyday lives.*

Turn the page for a sneak preview of
THE MAVERICK PREACHER
by
Victoria Bylin

*Love Inspired Historical—love and
faith throughout the ages*

Mr. Blue looked into her eyes with silent understanding and she wondered if he, too, had struggled with God's ways. The slash of his brow looked tight with worry, and his whiskers were too stubbly to be permanent. Adie thought about his shaving tools and wondered when he'd used them last. Her new boarder would clean up well on the outside, but his heart remained a mystery. She needed to keep it that way. The less she knew about him, the better.

"Good night," she said. "Bessie will check you in the morning."

"Before you go, I've been wondering…"

"About what?"

"The baby… Who's the mother?"

Adie raised her chin. "I am."

Earlier he'd called her "Miss Clarke" and she hadn't corrected him. The flash in his eyes told her that he'd assumed she'd given birth out of wedlock. Adie resented being judged, but she counted it as the price of protecting Stephen. If Mr. Blue chose to condemn her, so be it. She'd done nothing for which to be ashamed. With their gazes locked, she waiting for the criticism that didn't come.

Instead he laced his fingers on top of the Bible. "Children are a gift, all of them."

"I think so, too."

He lightened his tone. "A boy or a girl?"

"A boy."

The man smiled. "He sure can cry. How old is he?"

Adie didn't like the questions at all, but she took pride in her son. "He's three months old." She didn't mention that he'd been born six weeks early. "I hope the crying doesn't disturb you."

"I don't care if it does."

He sounded defiant. She didn't understand. "Most men would be annoyed."

"The crying's better than silence…. I know."

Adie didn't want to care about this man, but her heart fluttered against her ribs. What did Joshua Blue know of babies and silence? Had he lost a wife? A child of his own? She wanted to express sympathy but couldn't. If she pried into his life, he'd pry into hers. He'd ask questions and she'd have to hide the truth. *Stephen was born too soon and his mother died. He barely survived. I welcome his cries, every one of them. They mean he's alive.*

With a lump in her throat, she turned to leave. "Good night, Mr. Blue."

"Good night."

A thought struck her and she turned back to his room. "I supposed I should call you Reverend."

He grimaced. "I'd prefer Josh."

* * * * *

*Don't miss this deeply moving Love Inspired Historical
story about a man of God who's lost his way and
the woman who helps him rediscover
his faith—and his heart.*
THE MAVERICK PREACHER
by Victoria Bylin
available February 2009.

And also look for
THE MARSHAL TAKES A BRIDE
by Renee Ryan,
*in which a lawman meets his match in a feisty
schoolteacher with marriage on her mind.*

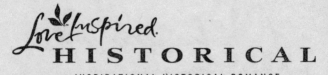

HISTORICAL

INSPIRATIONAL HISTORICAL ROMANCE

Adelaide Clark has worked hard to raise her young son on her own, and Boston minister Joshua Blue isn't going to break up her home. As she grows to trust Joshua, Adie sees he's only come to make amends for his past. Yet Joshua's love sparks a hope for the future that Adie thought was long dead—a future with a husband by her side.

Look for

The Maverick Preacher

by

VICTORIA BYLIN

*Available February 2009
wherever books are sold.*

Steeple
Hill®

LIH82805

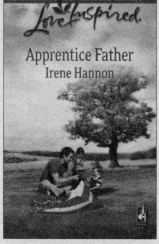

REQUEST YOUR FREE BOOKS!

2 FREE INSPIRATIONAL NOVELS
PLUS 2
FREE
MYSTERY GIFTS

Love Inspired.

YES! Please send me 2 FREE Love Inspired® novels and my 2 FREE mystery gifts (gifts are worth about $10). After receiving them, if I don't wish to receive any more books, I can return the shipping statement marked "cancel". If I don't cancel, I will receive 4 brand-new novels every month and be billed just $4.24 per book in the U.S. or $4.74 per book in Canada, plus 25¢ shipping and handling per book and applicable taxes, if any*. That's a savings of over 20% off the cover price! I understand that accepting the 2 free books and gifts places me under no obligation to buy anything. I can always return a shipment and cancel at any time. Even if I never buy another book, the two free books and gifts are mine to keep forever.

113 IDN ERXA   313 IDN ERWX

Name _____ (PLEASE PRINT)

Address _____ Apt. #

City _____ State/Prov. _____ Zip/Postal Code

Signature (if under 18, a parent or guardian must sign)

Order online at www.LoveInspiredBooks.com

Or mail to Steeple Hill Reader Service:

IN U.S.A.: P.O. Box 1867, Buffalo, NY 14240-1867
IN CANADA: P.O. Box 609, Fort Erie, Ontario L2A 5X3

Not valid to current subscribers of Love Inspired books.

Want to try two free books from another series?
Call 1-800-873-8635 or visit www.morefreebooks.com

* Terms and prices subject to change without notice. N.Y. residents add applicable sales tax. Canadian residents will be charged applicable provincial taxes and GST. Offer not valid in Quebec. This offer is limited to one order per household. All orders subject to approval. Credit or debit balances in a customer's account(s) may be offset by any other outstanding balance owed by or to the customer. Please allow 4 to 6 weeks for delivery. Offer available while quantities last.

Your Privacy: Steeple Hill Books is committed to protecting your privacy. Our Privacy Policy is available online at www.SteepleHill.com or upon request from the Reader Service. From time to time we make our lists of customers available to reputable third parties who may have a product or service of interest to you. If you would prefer we not share your name and address, please check here. ☐

LIREG08R

Love Inspired

TITLES AVAILABLE NEXT MONTH

Don't miss these four stories on sale January 27, 2009.

APPRENTICE FATHER by Irene Hannon
With an orphaned niece and nephew depending on him, commitment-shy Clay Adams calls upon nanny Cate Shepard to save them all. With God's help and her kind, nurturing ways, Cate may be able to ease the children into their new life. And her love could give lone-wolf Clay the forever family he deserves.

THEIR SMALL-TOWN LOVE by Arlene James
Eden, OK

A high school reunion means a trip home for new Christian Ivy Villard…to mend some fences. Past mistakes await her in tiny Eden, Oklahoma—like her former high school sweetheart, Ryan Jeffords. Yet a second chance at love is waiting for them, if they're brave enough to take it.

A COWBOY'S HEART by Brenda Minton
A lot of folks depend on ex-rodeo star Clint Cameron, including his twin four-year-old nephews. So why can't his stubborn neighbor, Willow Michaels, accept a little help with her bull-raising business? Clint's got a lot more than advice to offer Willow, if only she'd look deep in his faithful, loving heart.

BLUEGRASS COURTSHIP by Allie Pleiter
Kentucky Corners

Rebuilding the church's storm-damaged preschool is easy for the celebrity host of TV's *Missionnovation*, Drew Downing. Rebuilding lovely hardware store owner Janet Bishop's faith in God and love may be a bit more challenging. But Drew is just the man for the job.

LICNMBPA0109